NO TIME FOR TEARS

A South African Story

Phyllis Owen

Published in 2009 by New Generation Publishing

CHAPTER ONE

It was in the year eighteen hundred and ninety two. Ten year old Kate de Ponselle looked back at the ship from which they had just embarked. Its silhouette loomed dark and eerily against the early morning sky. The ghostly sound of lapping water made her shiver, even though the air was warm. She snuggled closer to her mother and father standing beside her on the wharf.

The long voyage from the Hoek of Holland had been a nightmare. There came over her a sense of forboding and she clung to her mother, desperate for a little reassurance that everything would now be all right.

A little over a year ago they had left their home in France. Kate's father was a blacksmith and worked at his trade in the small town of le Eglise on the outskirts of Paris, where Kate had been born. His blacksmith shop had been near to a cavalry barracks which provided him with a considerable amount of work. Suddenly, and quite unexpectedly, the cavalry vacated the barracks which were taken over by a regiment of Moroccan infantry. The business which had been in the de Ponselle family for centuries, slumped. Papa was offered a position in a blacksmith shop in Utrecht, Holland, and moved there with his family.

Prior to leaving their home in France, Papa had discussed with Mama the idea of going to South Africa. Several families in le Eglise had left to make a new life there. But the offer of employment in Utrecht had seemed good at the time and it was only when they arrived they discovered that the house in which they were to live was only a ramshackle hovel. Also, the owner of the business was a hard taskmaster and Papa's working hours were long and hard. Eleven months later, during which time Mama had been very ill, they took up the challenge to emmigrate to South Africa, the land of prospects, where they hoped to make a better life for themselves.

Mama put her arm around Kate's waist and kissed her on the top of her head. Kate was exceptionally small for her age and her dark lustrous blue eyes looked large in her thin serious little face which was surrounded by thick, dark hair worn in two pigtails.

Kate's mother, also very slender and short, had a beautiful face surrounded by the same dark hair which she wore in a bun on the nape of her neck. She was frail and weak from the fever that ravaged through the ship during their long, tiresome and at times, terrifying voyage. Many had succombed to the fever and were buried at sea. Kate recalled how ill her mother had been and clasped her hand. For several weeks she was afraid that her mother would die. She looked up into her pale face, its paleness emphasised by the black dress she was wearing.

Although Kate was a replica of her mother, she was wiry and strong.

'It won't be long now,' Papa said, smiling, as if to himself.'

He was of medium height, broad shouldered and tremenduously strong. His dark eyes were keen and piercing and at that moment they shone with excitement.

'Kate, my sweet,' he continued, 'at long last we've reached our destination. It's wonderful to breathe fresh air again after so many weeks in that stale musty atmosphere of the ship. I don't think I'll ever forget that crowded, badly lit saloon below the deck.

Kate knew only too well what he meant. The passengers had only been permitted to the deck for an hour each day, but, as the ship had been buffeted by storms during most of the voyage, this privilege had seldom been available to them.

Kate looked uncertainly about her. The wharf where they stood was a bustle of activity. Short bare footed yellow-skinned men wearing tattered shirts and trousers and who spoke in a strange clicking language, were loading large bales of merchandise on to oxwagons.

The sun was climbing high into the sky . It was only when the warm sun gradually soaked into her body that she began to relax.

Suddenly a man's voice called out, 'Monsieur de Ponselle! Monsieur Pierre de Ponselle......'

Papa raised his hand. 'Yes, I'm here,' he shouted in French, looking about him.

A tall bearded man with something of a gypsy look about him was hastening towards them. As he pushed his way through the milling crowd, Kate noticed that he had large capable hands and light blue twinkling eyes. He was wearing a blue shirt with a scarlet neckerchief and black trousers tucked into long knee length boots.

'Monsieur Phillipe Duval?' asked Papa.

The man nodded, smiling.

'We're happy to meet you,' went on Papa. 'This is my wife, Catherine, and my daughter, Kate. I'm glad you received my letter.'

'Welcome! Welcome!' Monsieur Duval bowed and kissed Mama's hand.

Mama smiled shyly at him.

'I've a carriage and pair to take you and your possessions to the van Soelens boarding house. Let me help you with that trunk.'

The de Ponselles had come with few possessions. All they owned was packed in one small trunk. In no time at all the trunk, Kate and her mother and father, were all safely on the carriage. As Monsieur Duval steered it along a dusty uneven road towards the town, he broke into snatches of French songs.

Kate smiled up at him. He made her feel happy inside.

The sun was now climbing high into the sky and as she looked up she saw the mountain for the first time. It was covered by a misty cloth that seemed to join it to the sky. It looked ethereal and mysterious. For a moment a little shiver of fear passed through her but as the warm sun gradually soaked into her body she relaxed. Their life must be better from now on, she thought. It just had to be. Certainly it couldn't be any worse.

'You don't have a mountain like that where you come from.' said Monsieur Duval, pointing.

'No!' exclaimed Papa. 'I've never seen anything like it before. It's truly magnificient!'

As they drove along Monsieur Duval's bubbling personality soon had them all laughing heartily.

'I'm sure you'll enjoy working in the blacksmith shop, Pierre,' he said, 'and the boarding house run by the van Soelens is good. Alie van Soelen likes the French and her cooking is oh, la, la.' He licked his lips appreciably and laughed. 'I've had many a good meal there.'

They drove along the road and Kate stared in wonder at the broad streets bordered by trees and seemingly endless rows of neat, white-washed houses. Her thoughts went back to those distant days and to their cramped little home in Utrecht with the front door that opened directly on to a narrow dirty street.

Monsieur Duval broke into Kate's thoughts. 'We're here,' he said, bringing the horses to a halt in front of a large white-washed single storey house with a flat roof and shuttered windows.

Kate stared in amazement. It looked so large! Steps led up to a veranda which ran the length of the front of the house. Monsieur Duval lifted her down from the carriage while Papa helped Mama to alight.

Just then the front door opened and a middle-aged, plump short woman, her round face wreathed in smiles, hastened down the steps to them. She moved so quickly it looked as if she were floating just above the ground.

'I'm Alie van Soelen,' she said, 'we welcome you to our land and hope you'll be very happy and that your stay with us will be pleasant.'

'Thank you for your kindness, Madam,' said Mama, in faltering Dutch.

In Holland, Kate and her parents had picked up a smattering of the language and were thus able to understand something of what their host was saying.

'My name's Alie,' insisted Mrs. Van Soelen, kindly.

'And mine's Catherine,' responded Mama.

Mr van Soelen hurried from the house. After warmly greeting them he said, 'Let me help you with your luggage.'

'This is all we have,' replied Papa, pointing to the trunk at the back of the carriage.

'Then I'll help you take it to your room.'

'I must go now, Pierre,' came in Monsieur Duval. 'I'll see you in the morning.'

'May I come to the shop this afternoon?' asked Papa, 'I'm looking forward to working again. My hands have become soft after the long sea voyage.'

Monsieur Duval nodded. 'Of course, I look forward to seeing you. If you continue down this road until the next corner and then turn left, you'll find the Smithy on the righthand side.' Bowing slightly, he added, 'Well good people, I must go now. By the way, Albert,' he turned to Mr van Soelen, 'did you manage to get those shoeing nails for me?'

'I expect them to be delivered to the store any time this afternoon,' replied Mr van Soelen.

'Good, good. Thank you, Albert.' Monsieur Duval turned, climbed on to the carriage and urged the horses forward.

They all walked up the steps to the front door with Papa and Mr van Soelen carrying the luggage. An old woman stepped on to the veranda. A tall, gangly youth of about thirteen, wearing knickerbrokers and a white cotton shirt, followed close behind her.

'Meet Ouma van Soelen,' said Tant Alie.'

Ouma was of medium height and very fat. She wore a dark print ankle-length dress. Over her ample skirt was a crisp white frilly pinafore. Her face was surrounded by silver hair and her blue eyes were warm and friendly.

'Welcome, the de Ponselle family,' she said.

'This is my son, Albert Junior,' put in Mr. Van Soelen, proudly, patting the youth on the back. 'We call him Junior for obvious reasons. It avoids confusion.'

Kate glanced at Junior for a moment without really seeing him. Then her eyes caught his. They were regarding her with amusement. A flash of annoyance swept through her. He had a smooth baby face and deep set brown eyes. His fair hair was streaked almost white by the sun and his skin was a golden brown.

Suddenly he burst out laughing. 'Don't look so cross, Katie. I won't eat you,' he said, in a mixture of French and Dutch.

'Now, Junior, no teasing,' said his mother, chuckling. 'He's a dreadful tease, Kate. Ignore him.'

Kate's face darkened. 'My name's not Katie, it's Kate,' she hissed.

A round-faced girl with blonde curly hair, about Kate's age, bounced towards them followed by a large black dog wagging its tail and barking excitedly.

Kate clung to her mother.

'Don't be frightened of the dog,' smiled Oom Albert, 'He's very tame.' Turning to the girl he added, 'Poppie, meet our new friends.' He put his arm around her waist. 'Poppie is the baby of the family and Wagter her faithful friend and hound.' He laughed.

Kate stared at Poppie. She wore a pretty blue printed dress that came to below her knees, with a white pinafore, stockings and black leather shoes. She greeted them shyly and came up to Kate. 'Hello,' she said, coyly, 'I hope we'll be friends. I have three sisters who are married and live far away and I'm glad you've come to live here.'

Kate warmed to her and smiled. 'I'm glad too,' she whispered.

'Poppie, take Kate to your room,' said Tant Alie. 'Pierre and Catherine, Albert will take you to your room. I'll see to the food. We'll have an early lunch today because I'm sure you must be hungry.'

Taking Kate by the hand, Poppie led her into the house. Laughing and talking, the others followed.

CHAPTER TWO

The front door led into a large hall with a high wooden ceiling. Kate caught her breath. There were a number of chairs, an oval-shaped table, an umbrella stand and an enormous grandfather clock. On the walls were paintings in thick dark frames. Kate recognised some of the Holland scenes with the dykes and windmills. Rooms led off on either side of the hall.

They passed through a doorway leading into a spacious dining room. The long table in the centre was set ready for a meal. There were also paintings and maps hanging on the walls and a barometer. Kate spied a pantry behind a large teak screen. The shelves were full of bottled fruit, jam and home made preserve. Off the dining room were the bedrooms.

Kate followed Poppie from room to room. She noticed that they were all spotlessly clean and neat. The wooden floors and furniture shone brightly and in each room were shelves full of pewter, brass and porcelain plates. The kitchen impressed Kate the most. It's delicious aromas reminded her that she hadn't eaten since the previous evening. The kitchen was almost as large as the dining room. Brass and copper pots and kettles gleamed in the sunlight that came streaming in through the open door and windows.

Poppie pointed to a room adjoining the kitchen. 'That's Ouma's room,' she said, hesitating, and then added, 'Let's go to our room.'

Kate was pleased she was to share a room with Poppie. It was the smallest room in the house. It had two beds, a large mahogany wardrobe, dressing table and an old oak chest. On the chest was a porcelain basin and water jug. The curtains were made of patchwork with matching bedspreads.

'How pretty!' gasped Kate.

'My Ouma and Mama made the curtains and bedspreads,' smiled Poppie, proudly. 'I helped a little. We collected odd bits of material from our friends and for months we sat and sewed whenever we could and last week they were ready for Papa to hang.'

'It's lovely!' exclaimed Kate. She felt happy and certain that everything was now going to go well for them. How could it not in this beautiful home.

'Your parents are in the room next door,' said Poppie, 'I'll take you to them.' Taking Kate by the hand, she led her into the passage. Pointing to a door she said, 'In there. I must go and help Mama. Come to the dining room as soon as you're ready.'

Kate nodded and tapped softly on the door.

'Come in,' called Mama.

Kate opened the door. The room was much larger than Poppie's. A big four poster bed with carved wooden pillars was set against the wall. It had rich maroon velvet drapings and a canopy. Next to the bed lay a kaross, a sheepskin rug. A double wardrobe, wash-stand with pewter basin and jug, a couch and a small table completed the furnishings. At the window hung heavy maroon velvet curtains.

'Come and sit on the soft bed, Kate my sweet,' called Papa, flopping down on it. He was almost swallowed up in all the bedding. 'I won't be able to get up in the mornings.' He laughed heartily.

Mama's eyes were sparkling. 'I'm so happy to be here,' she breathed.

Kate responded to her parents pleasure with a smile that lit up her face.

'Let's go,'said Papa, jumping up from the bed. 'We must not keep anyone waiting. I'm hungry. I can't wait to eat some good homemade food.'

'No badly salted meat and stale biscuits,'chuckled Mama.

'I hope we never have to eat another piece of salt beef as long as we live,' groaned Papa.

As they walked down the passage they heard the murmur of voices and the clatter of crockery. Delicious smells came to meet them when they opened the dining room door. The family were already at the table.

'Sit down, Monsieur, Madam, Katie,' said Junior, jumping up and pulling out three chairs for them.
'Thank you,'said Mama and Papa as they sat down. Kate stood back waiting for Junior to pass, but he remained behind her chair.

'Come, Katie, sit. Why are you waiting?' he sniggered.

Embarrassed and annoyed Kate quickly sat down as he pushed the chair under her. Walking round the table he sat directly opposite her.

Mr van Soelen coughed and held up his hand. They all closed their eyes and he said the grace.

The meal was very good. Never had Kate tasted such meat before. It had been cut into small pieces and mixed with the vegetables. When she had finished she could not believe that she had managed to eat so much.

'Would anyone like a second helping?' asked Tant Alie.

'Yes, please,' replied Junior.

Kate threw him a disgusted glance.

'What about you Pierre, Catherine?' enquired Tant Alie.

Kate's father laughed and looked across at Mama, who shook her head. 'Yes, please, I'd love some more. Tres bien! The food's good.' He laughed and added, 'At this rate I shall surely grow sideways.'

The months passed quickly by. Kate was happier than she had ever been before. There was a healthy colour in her cheeks and the underlying sense of forboding and doubt that had so often haunted her gradually disappeared.

Each afternoon, after school, Ouma gave Kate and Poppie sewing lessons and taught them how to knit. Mama helped Tant Alie in the house and Papa enjoyed his work with Monsieur Duval who, together with his wife and two little girls, was a frequent visitor. Each time he called he would sing a French song especially for Kate. He was also an excellent story teller and often had them in fits of laughter.

One story that Kate particularly enjoyed concerned the time he was serving as a conscript in the French Army at Dijon. Whilst preparing for a full dress parade he discovered, to his horror, that someone had stolen his helmet. He searched frantically for it without success and was forced to parade with his regiment, bareheaded. During the inspection the sergeant berated him for coming to the parade ground without his helmet.

'Where's your helmet, Duval?' he shouted.

'If it pleases the Sergeant,' replied Monsieur Duval, 'It has been stolen.'

'It does not please me, Duval,' shouted the Sergeant, who was by now beside himself with rage. 'I don't mind where you get another helmet from, even if you have to steal one. Whatever you do, you must not come on parade bareheaded, do you understand?'

'Oui, Sergeant, I understand very well.'

When the parade was over, Monsieur Duval sat on his bed in the barracks dejectedly pondering his predicament. A new helmet would cost four francs, eight centimes. Nearly a months pay!

'What did you do, Monsieur?' Poppie asked.

Monsieur Duval sat back in his chair and grinned. 'I took the Sergeant's advice and stole a helmet.'

'But,' Kate interjected, 'didn't that mean that one of your friends would be without his helmet?'

Monsieur Duval burst out laughing. 'Not in the least,' he replied, 'the Sergeant was no friend of mine.'

'I don't understand,' began Kate.

'I stole the Sergeant's helmet.'

'One thing about you, Phillipe, you never allow the truth to stand in the way of a good story,' chuckled Oom Albert.

Kate attended school with the van Soelen children. It was held in the large loft of a house only a block and a half away from their home. When they heard the bell ringing they would hurry down the road and arrive just in time for lessons. She hadn't liked school at the beginning. Apart from the fact that she knew only a smattering of Dutch, there were so many children and she felt shy and nervous when they teased her because she was so small. To Kate's surprise Junior quickly became her protector and gradually the teasing ceased.

At first the lessons were hard to follow for the teacher only spoke in Dutch and English, but Poppie helped her at home. As the months passed Kate found it easier to understand and became fluent in the languages.

Poppie's warmth and generosity had been of considerable help to her in settling into this new and strange country. She hoped with all her heart that she would never be separated from her.

Even though Junior protected her from the teasing at school he was a trial to her at home. Finally she resorted to ignoring him and much to her delight his unkind remarks ceased. In later years she often wished that other problems that came her way could be overcome by simply ignoring them.

It was the weekend and Ouma called Poppie and Kate. 'I want to show you how to make a pinafore. Sit on the bench, girls,' Ouma said, 'and I'll sit between you. I've already cut out the pinafores and will show you how to sew them neatly.

She gave the girls long strips of soft white cotton material. 'These are the frills,'she explained. 'We must hem them first.' Ouma threaded the needles and passed one to each of the girls. She showed Kate and Poppie how to hem in fine even small stitches. Every now and again she inspected their work. Once she was satisfied that they knew what to do she sat back on the bench, her head against the wall.

'Are you going to tell us a story of long ago, Ouma?' Poppie asked.

Ouma laughed. 'Yes.'

Ouma looked at their eager young faces. 'As you have learned at school,' she began, 'the Portugese were the first to discover the sea-route to the East by sailing around Africa and past our fair Cape. They became very wealthy trading in spices, rugs, silks, ivory: all things that were in great demand in Europe. The Portugese kept the route to India a secret. Finally a

Hollander, Jan van Linschoten, who, because he had lived in Portugal for many years, was allowed to travel in a Portugese ship. He kept a record of the winds they encountered and the harbours they called at along the way. In this way he was able to work out the route. When he returned, after six years, his notes were published for all to read. Later, some Dutch merchants formed a company to sail the route. Cornelius de Houtman was the first Dutchman to try and he reached the East Indies. He took back spices to Holland. Soon the English and French ships were passing the Cape on their voyages to and from the East. The Portugese never tried to land at the Cape because of the bad storms. Also, they feared the native tribes. But the Dutch, French and English navigators often went ashore to get fresh water. The English and Dutch used the Cape as a post office.'

'How did they do that!'exclaimed Poppie.

Ouma laughed. 'They wrapped letters in oil-cloth and left them under a large flat stone for crews of other ships to collect and take them to their destinations.' Ouma stopped to inspect Kate's work. 'That's good, Kate,' she said. 'You are a quick learner. How are you doing Poppie?'

'I'm trying hard, Ouma. I don't want to pull it out.'

Ouma smiled. 'Maybe the story is putting you off.'

'No, no, Ouma, please carry on,' Poppie insisted.

'All right, but not a long one. Near Table Bay, there was a ship wreck. at the Cape. A Dutch ship, the Haarlem, was driven ashore during a violent storm and had to be abandoned. The crew reached the shore safely with provisions and some of the cargo. Two English ships helped to take some of the crew back home but sixty men remained under the command of Leendert Janssen. They had to wait many months for the next Dutch ship.

'They built a fort for protection and sunk a well for water. They had rescued vegetable seeds and garden tools from the ship so they planted a garden. The Hottentots watched them curiously. After several months they brought large numbers of cattle and sheep to exchange for articles the men had salvaged from the ship.'

'Ouma!' exclaimed Kate, suddenly, 'My cotton's finished.'

'Oogh, Kate, you sew quickly,' said Poppie, surprised. 'I still have a long thread.'

Ouma chuckled. She threaded Kate's needle and gave it to her. 'I'll carry on for a short while as it is getting late. 'About a year later the stranded men were taken back to Holland and Janssen put the idea to the company that a refreshment station be started at the Cape. He also suggested a hospital be built for sick sailors. After a long discussion it was agreed to establish a refreshment station and the man to command it was none other than our famous man of history...'

'Jan van Riebeeck!' shouted Poppie, excitedly. 'We learned that at school.

'None other,' laughed Ouma, 'and the name of his ships?'

'Reiger, Dromedaris and Goede Hoop,' Poppie came back, a broad smile on her face.

Ouma laughed. 'Quite right. Now I think you need a bit of sunshine.'

After packing away their sewing, Kate and Poppie ran into the back garden. Wagter joined them, barking excitedly. It then occurred to Kate that Poppie was the first real friend she had ever had, someone she could trust and confide in. She also realised that Poppie's warmth and generosity had been of considerable help to her in settling in this new and strange country. She hoped with all her heart that they would never be separated.

CHAPTER THREE

Poppie had a bad cold. Kate sat with her in the bedroom trying, not very successfully, to cheer her up. Kate read her a story but before she came to the end, Poppie was fast asleep. 'Poor Poppie,' she sighed. 'Your nose looks so red and sore.'

'Kate!' whispered Mama at the door, 'Come, let's go for a walk. A good sleep will help Poppie to overcome her illness and a dose of fresh air will do us good.'

Kate's face lit up as she gazed at Mama's lovely face, pale against the darkness of her hair. She was still too thin, but her eyes were bright and sparkling as if she were nursing some hidden secret.

They made their way through the front door. Whilst they were walking down the street Mama tucked her arm into Kate's. With a light step they walked up a small rise not far from the house, where they had a view of the yellow beach and the ocean. The ocean looked calm enough, but every now and again, large waves somersaulted on to the beach in a whirl of white foam. It excited them to watch the waves as they relentlessly rushed forwards and backwards. Kate loved the way the seagulls wheeled and dived and let out their desolate cries. They flew so effortlessly in the sky hardly beating their large wings. There was something so peaceful and reassuring about the surroundings that chased away any worries she may have. She licked her lips trying to taste the saltiness of the sea air.

Mama hugged her. 'Time to go back. I must helpTant Alie.'

They had been living in the Cape just on eighteen months when Monsieur Duval was killed in an accident. He was shoeing a high spirited horse when there was a sudden noise from outside. The horse reared and crushed him against the wall. He died instantly. Monsieur Duval's blacksmith shop was sold and as the new owners did not need Papa, they asked him to leave.

One evening, a week after the funeral, Papa rushed into the room, his eyes shining from excitement. He told Mama and Kate that he had met a farmer in town whose name was Hendrik van Heerden. As he and his wife had no children and he was getting on in years, he found running his farm on his own, too much to handle and asked Papa to be his assistant.

Kate's heart sank because she didn't want to leave the van Soelens, but she pretended to be happy for his sake. She knew being a farmer was what Papa had always wanted. Mama was smiling.

Kate couldn't hide her shock and dismay when Papa told them the farm was in the Free State Republic and that they were leaving in two days time. 'It is such a long, long, way,' she protested. 'We won't ever see Poppie and Ouma van Soelen again. She burst into tears.

Mama put her arms around her and said quietly, 'We'll miss them too. They've been generous and kind, but we'll come back for a holiday one day.'

She brightened at these words. 'Oh, Mama, will we?'

'Of course we will,'she promised and then added, 'Don't be frightened of change, Kate. As long as we are together we can surely face anything. We've proved it in the past.'

She nodded, but deep down a sense of depression descended on her. When she told Poppie she burst into tears and they clung together.

Kate helped Mama with the preparations for the journey and the time passed all too quickly. She felt as if she was living in a dream world. For nothing seemed real. When she told Poppie they were leaving they clung together, crying bitterly, promising to visit each other as soon as they were able to do so. But deep down Kate knew this would never be.

She couldn't rid herself of the dull ache in her heart. She had hoped that in coming to South Africa their life would be better. Their lives had changed and she had come to know real happiness, but that happiness was all too illusive.

'Don't be sad, my dear,' Mama told her when she saw her downcast face. 'There's a good reason for everything that happens to us. We'll always have pleasant memories of our stay here. Something to look back on with pleasure.' She looked at Kate and smiled warmly. 'Remember, life is full of changes.'

'Yes, Mama,' she replied without conviction.

Mama chuckled and took her hands in hers. 'I've some good news for you, she said mysteriously.

Kate's curiosity was aroused. She looked at Mama's lovely face. It was still too thin. But her eyes were bright and sparkling as if hiding some secret. 'One of these days you'll have a brother or sister,' she said, chuckling.

Kate stared at her open-mouthed and then burst out excitedly, 'Oh, Mama, how wonderful! It's something I've always longed for, to have a brother or sister.'

The train left the following evening on its journey northwards. Kate's heart sunk at the thought of, once again, facing the unknown. She hung out of the window and waved until the train made its way around a curve, like an iron snake, and she could no longer see the van Soelens.

Sitting down on the hard wooden bench beside the window, she watched the mountains, dim against the evening sky, slowly pass by. Two ivy clad trees loomed eerily, like tombstones, out of the darkness. They looked grim and forbidding in the moonlight.

She slept fitfully on a hard wooden bunk and in her waking moments the incessant clickety clack, clickety clack of the wheels sent a chill of fear running down her spine.

The next morning, while Papa was still sleeping, she and Mama watched the sun rise over the Karoo. It's long rays reached high into the sky. The scenery had changed, the parched land was criss-crossed with dry river beds and the countryside, flat and unchanging, was covered with a thick carpet of kraalbos. There were occasional granite outcrops that formed sudden steep-sided hills called kopjes and they could be seen far in the distance. Herds of buck grazed peacefully near the railway line.

'Those are springbuck,' whispered Mama. 'See their white, black and brown colouring?'

'They're so small!' Kate exclaimed, surprised. She had only seen pictures of springbuck and thought they would be much larger.

Mama chuckled and kissed her on the cheek. 'I'm sure we are going to be very happy on the farm.'

Kate stared at her for a moment, but couldn't speak and continued to look out of the window. Here and there small white-washed farm houses dotted the veld. One such farm house, its white-washed walls sparkling in the sunlight, was situated close to the railway line. A tall bearded man was herding some sheep into a large pen and as we passed he looked up and waved.

The remainder of the journey to the Free State Republic was long and tiring and Kate lost all sense of time. Finally, after what seemed an eternity, Papa woke her up early one morning and announced, 'We've arrived in Bloemfontein!' She could hear the excitement in his voice and was surprised to find that she too was looking forward to seeing their new home.

Papa helped Mama and Kate from the train and they waited on the platform, huddled together against the cold wind, while Papa collected their trunk from the guard's van.

Kate felt confused and shivered uncontrollably, pulling her shawl tightly around her shoulders. She had a sudden longing for Ouma, Poppie and Tant Alie. She clung to Mama.

'Good morning, Pierre de Ponselle!' came a gruff voice from behind them.

Kate turned and stared at a tall bearded man. He had a face which fell easily into a smile, with eyes so gentle it was as if they could see right through you. He removed his wide brimmed hat to reveal a head of thick black hair streaked with grey.

Papa hurried up to us carrying our trunk on his shoulder. 'Good morning, Hendrik van Heerden!' he responded. 'Meet my wife, Catherine and daughter, Kate.'

'How do you do, Mam, Kate!'

He shook hands with Mama.

'Pleased to meet you, Mr van Heerden,' she greeted in Dutch, smiling.

Like Kate, Papa was almost fluent in the language. Her Mama wasn't bad but she stumbled over some words and with her strong French accent the words were difficult to understand, but she was improving. Kate or Papa helped her. Kate had learned a lot from Tant Alie and Ouma van Soelen. They only spoke French when they were in their room.

Mr van Heerden stooped down and shook hands with Kate.

She smiled shyly.

'I've a carriage waiting, and please call me Hendrik.' He inclined his head towards the station yard.

Kate studied him closely. He was well built and much taller than Papa. His oval-shaped beard and large moustache were streaked with grey and his penetrating eyes were as black as the night. There was something about his quiet but assured manner that gave her a feeling of confidence. He wore a leather coat and breeches with a home spun cotton shirt and had a red hankerchief tied around his neck.

He looked at them and smiled. 'Clara, my wife, is excited about having another woman on the farm.'

Kate noticed a note of warmth in his voice as he helped her into the cart. She leaned back against the wooden seat lost in thoughts of the Cape and was brought back to the present by Papa suddenly crying out, 'What a country! Kilometres of nothing! Space, glorious space!'

Uncle Hendrik laughed heartily. 'When you come to understand this country you'll find it is the most beautiful country in the world, but you have to know how to handle it because it can also break your heart.'

Kate stared at the wild and yet somehow beautiful country. Here and there were ploughed fields. Everything about the place, the people, the horses, the land, was larger than life.

They made their way along an uneven dirt road. The morning sun glinted on the dry grass which grew in thick clumps. The only shade was cast by the gnarled and twisted branches of umbrella-shaped thorn trees. It was so different from the lush greenery of the Cape.

After travelling for about an hour, they came to a stony section of the road and the rattling of the carriage wheels made conversation impossible. A few minutes later they reached a tree-lined drive leading off the road. On a wooden post was painted the words, 'Aangenaam' and underneath, 'H J van Heerden'.

'The name of your farm?' queried Papa.

'Yes,' replied Uncle Hendrik, with a chuckle. 'It means pleasant, agreeable.'

Kate watched with bated breath as they emerged from the trees at the end of the drive and gasped with pleasure when she saw a white-walled farmhouse glistening in the sunlight surrounded by a picket fence covered with rose bushes. It had a thatched roof and at one end a stairway led up to a loft. A few steps reached up to a verandah that ran along the front of the house.

Uncle Hendrik drew on the reigns and brought the two horses to a halt. Kate was stiff from the journey and glad to be lifted down from the carriage by Uncle Hendrik.

The front door opened and a tall, grey-haired woman came towards them with hands outstretched, her face wreathed in smiles. There was about her an unmistakable air of refinement. She was wearing a dull-coloured cotton dress and a crisp white pinafore. Her long lair was parted in the centre and tied back in plaits. Something about her commanded instant respect. With bright eyes darting from face to face, she came towards them smiling. 'You must be Catherine and this is Kate.' She smiled at her. 'How glad I am to meet you.'

'My wife, Clara,' introduced Uncle Hendrik, proudly.

Aunt Clara kissed Mama and then Kate and, after shaking Papa's hand, led us into the house. A large black dog ran towards them. Kate clung to Mama's arm.

'Brakkies, out!' shouted Uncle Hendrik. Turning to Kate he said, 'He won't bite you. He's so big and that's what makes him look vicious. But he's harmless.'

The house was warm and comfortably furnished. We sat round the large table in the kitchen drinking coffee and eating hot drop scones with homemade butter and jam.

'You'll be living in the first house we built for ourselves when coming to this farm,' smiled Aunt Clara. 'I'm sure you'll be very comfortable here.'

'I know we will,' Mama replied, her face beaming.

'I'm glad the house will, at last, be occupied,' Aunt Clara continued.'Ten years back my cousin and his wife were about to join us on the farm, but he went hunting with a few friends the week before they were to leave,' she shook her head sadly, 'somehow he tripped and shot himself. Very sad.'

Uncle Hendrik broke in, 'It'll be wonderful having a child about the place, hey Clara?'

'In a few months there'll be another,' put in Mama, smiling shyly, her face scarlet.

'Really?' exclaimed Uncle Hendrik. 'Wonderbaar!'

After they had eaten, Uncle Hendrik said, 'We'll take you to your new home.'

They followed him out of the kitchen, down the steps of the back verandah and through a wire mesh gate. About a hundred metres away stood the loveliest little house Kate had ever seen. It was also painted white and had a thatched roof. Small windows were set deeply in the thick walls.

Aunt Clara opened the front door and they walked into a square-shaped living room furnished with wooden chairs and there were thick white karossess on a floor of beaten mud. Off the room were three doors. One led into the kitchen which also served as a dining room and the other two led into bedrooms. The smaller of the two was for Kate. To the end of her days she was sure she would never forget the thrill of that moment when she first set eyes on her room, her very own room. It was as though she had awakened from a beautiful dream. In the room was a bedstead and a large wooden dressing table. In one corner was a curtained enclosure.

She looked enquiringly at Mama.

'For your clothes,' she whispered.

The curtains and bedspread were made of patchwork. Even though the room was not as pretty as Poppie's, she loved it. 'It's the most beautiful room I've ever seen,' she exclaimed.

Everyone laughed.

'You're such a dear little thing,' said Aunt Clara, bending down and hugging her.

Mama and Papa's room was much larger and had a large bed covered with karosses. There was a wardrobe, dressing table and oak chest. The kitchen was small but adequate for their needs. It contained a wooden table, some chairs and a cupboard. A fire crackled in the stove. On top of the stove stood a coffee pot. A thin whisp of steam came out of the spout. Kate could smell the heavy aroma of the coffee beans.

'Coffee is ready at all times in a farmer's kitchen,' explained Aunt Clara.

Just then a large brown dog with long legs, came bounding into the kitchen, its tail wagging. For some reason Kate couldn't understand, she didn't feel the least bit frightened.

'This is Langbeen,' laughed Uncle Hendrik. 'He's yours if you want him.'

Langbeen came up to Kate, licked her hand and snuggled his head against her waist. He gave a few short barks to show his pleasure. Kate took to him immediately.

'Can we keep him, Papa?' she pleaded.

'Of course,' smiled Papa. 'He's already chosen you to be his mistress. It'll mean that you must feed him and see to his needs.'

'Oh I will,' she promised.

'I've filled the grocery cupboard,' explained Aunt Clara,' and will send the milk, eggs and meat later.'

'You are too good to us,' cried Mama. 'This is all so unbelievable.'

'Yes,' agreed Papa, then turning to Uncle Hendrik, added, 'I would like very much to see the lands.'

'Good!' replied Uncle Hendrik. 'Let's go.'

Papa followed him out through the kitchen door. Moments later, a plump black woman, in her early twenties, came into the kitchen. She wore a dark blue ankle length dress with a white cap and apron of course linen. Her face was smooth and shining and when she smiled she showed a set of even white teeth.

'This is Mintjie,' explained Aunt Clara. 'She'll help you in the house. Her cooking is good. I trained her myself.'

Mintjie looked at them and smiled shyly.

'Hello, Mintjie,' greeted Mama in her way. 'I'm pleased to meet you.'

'Mintjie, help these people to pack their things away,' said Aunt Clara, 'I'll see you later, Catherine,' she added.

Mama nodded and Aunt Clara left.

Kate took Langbeen into the back garden and stared curiously around her. The garden was surrounded by a low stone wall. On one side was a small vegetable garden and at the far end, a row of peach and apricot trees. About two hundred metres away from the wall was a dam surrounded by willow trees. Near the dam were two wooden enclosures into which the sheep and cows were herded at night. Beyond the dam was a cluster of mud huts with flat roofs where the farm labourers lived. Just ahead of them Kate could see the sheep, cows and a few goats, grazing on a slope.

She felt a surge of happiness and smiled contentedly, sitting down on the low wall. How could she have dreaded coming here? She felt as if her heart was about to burst with joy. Then she became aware of a strange chill coming over her and she told herself angrily not to be so stupid. She trembled in spite of herself.

CHAPTER FOUR

Kate's apprehension soon disappeared and, as the months passed, they adapted themselves to their surroundings and became happily absorbed with their new way of life. The years spent in France and Holland and the long sea voyage slipped into some distant recess of Kate's memory. She often thought with pleasure of the time spent in the Cape and of Poppie and her family, but she was quite reconciled with her new life on the farm. The dark fears that had haunted her for so long left and she would go for longer and longer walks in the veld with her faithful friend, Langbeen. She loved him dearly and often told him about her innermost thoughts and dreams. He would listen attentively, turning his head this way and that as if he understood everything she was saying to him. Now and again Brakkies would join them but most times he went into the lands with Papa and Uncle Hendrik. Kate had become accustomed to life on the farm as if she had been born there.

Kate and Mintjie were good friends and she often visited Mintjie's home and her two children, meeting her husband, the Chief, and his other wives. Mintjie was the youngest wife and to Kate the most beautiful. There were numerous children of all ages living in the group of huts. Each wife had her own hut where she lived with her children. The older boys worked for Uncle Hendrik on the farm, some in the lands while others herded the sheep, goats and cows. The girls helped the women to clean the huts. They also cooked the food and cared for the smaller children.

One of the wives, Lena, worked for Aunt Clara. She was tall and had rather a generous bottom. Kate didn't like or trust her, but Aunt Clara said she was a hard worker and learnt fast. There was something about her that Kate found disturbing. She noticed that whenever something went wrong in the household like, for instance, if Aunt Clara broke a cup or basin, or if the porridge bubbled over on to the floor, Lena would smile smugly to herself.

One afternoon, when Kate was helping Aunt Clara in the kitchen, Aunt Clara almost stepped on a baby night adder. Fortunately the snake was as petrified as Aunt Clara and slithered underneath a cupboard. Even though Lena screamed in horror and fled from the house, Kate noticed a gleam of satisfaction on her face. Kate couldn't understand why because Aunt Clara treated her well and often gave her clothing and extra food for her family.

Aunt Clara, with the help of a broom handle, soon removed the snake from the kitchen and into the yard, where it was killed.

Every morning Mama taught Kate to write and spell words found in the Bible. Books were scarce. She had learned much from the school in the Cape, but she enjoyed her lessons with Mama. In the afternoons she helped Aunt Clara to make butter from the rich milk of the cows. She also helped to make soap from the ashes of the kanna bush and candles from melted sheep's fat. To make the candles, fat was poured into a small round tin and a piece of rag was used for a wick.

Kate loved working with Aunt Clara. Aunt Clara said she was a keen student and quick to learn. Kate came to love her and Uncle Hendrik almost as much as her parents.

One afternoon, while Kate was sitting with Mama in the kitchen, Langbeen came bouncing into the house.

'Take that enormous animal out of here,' laughed Mama.

'You want me to take you for a walk?' Kate asked, putting her arms around him.

He licked her face, whining excitedly.

She ran outside with Langbeen at her heels and hastened towards the open veld. After a while she stopped and looked about her at the neat white-washed buildings of the farm and of the countryside that stretched endlessly into the distance, bathed in the warm November sunshine. A strong breeze ruffled the drooping branches of the willows bordering the dam. She looked at the fluffy white clouds gently rolling across the sky. Langbeen came up to her and whimpered. She stroked his head and whispered, 'This is where I belong. I ask for nothing more of life. I want to stay here forever.'

As if comprending her words Langbeen barked and offered her his paw. She laughed and shook it.

A few days later, as Kate walked into the kitchen, she saw Mama gripping the back of a chair with both hands, her face contorted and deathly pale. Kate cried out with alarm and rushed to her side. Mama took a deep breath. 'Kate, don't look so alarmed, my dear. The baby's coming, that's all.' She spoke in a series of short gasps. 'Go and call Aunt Clara and find Papa. He's down in the lands. Tell him to come at once.' She smiled wanly and took her hand. 'First help me to the bedroom.'

She did as she was told and carefully sat her mother down on the large bed. As Kate looked at her, a great tenderness washed over her. Then, with fear putting wings to her feet, she first ran to tell Aunt Clara that the baby was coming and then hurried to the lands to find Papa. Langbeen followed her, barking excitedly.

Kate felt a strange mixture of emotions. One minute she was happy the baby would soon be born and the next, a wave of terror came over her and she trembled. Mama looked deathly pale and was obviously in great pain.

Kate found Papa ploughing in a field on the other side of the dam. 'Papa!' she shouted, 'Mama says to come quickly. The baby is coming.'

Papa gave her a startled look before winding the reins around one handle of the plough. Then he rushed to the house leaving her behind to follow him. By the time Kate arrived, it was a hive of activity.

Aunt Clara was in the kitchen giving instructions to Mintjie and Papa. 'I'll need plenty of hot water so keep it on the boil,'she said. When she saw Kate, she added, 'Be a good girl and help your Papa. Everything will be just fine.'

Kate sat in silence while the hours passed slowly by. Aunt Clara had asked Mintjie to come and help her so it left her and Papa to make sure the water was kept boiling on the stove. Every now and again Kate would hear a stifled cry coming from the bedroom and the low murmur of voices. Once Aunt Clara came out and reported cheerfully that everything was going according to plan and that there was no need for them to be concerned. She smiled and gave Kate a hug.

Kate was bursting with questions. She wanted to know why the baby was taking so long to arrive and could she not see Mama just for a moment?

'When he or she is good and ready to announce its arrival it will do so and not before,' she told Kate, not unkindly, 'and as soon as everything is over you'll be able to see your mother.' With that she left the kitchen.

Kate looked at Papa questioningly.

He shook his head. 'I don't know the answer,' he said, almost apologetically, 'But you also took a long time to come into the world.'

Kate relaxed a little but couldn't shake off a feeling of panic. Her legs were trembling as she walked to the stove to move the kettle to one side as it had began to boil over. In a daze she made her and Papa a mug of coffee and sat at the table sipping the hot liquid in silence, each with their own thoughts.

Finally, much later that night, Papa suggested, wearily, that she go to bed.

'There's nothing more to do and no point in you missing your sleep. I'll call you when it's all over and then you can come and see the baby.' There were dark shadows of exhaustion under his eyes.

Kate didn't protest for she was tired and hardly able to keep her eyes open. She crawled into bed and dropped off to sleep almost immediately her head touched the pillow.

A few hours later she awoke suddenly, all instincts alert, with an uneasy sensation that something was seriously amiss. Her brain was firing on all cylinders and her toes tingled. There was a bustle of activity in the adjoining bedroom, and then silence. Kate heard the brief cry of a baby. A door closed and footsteps faded into the night. The silence was forbidding in its stillness and seemed to hold a threat of tragedy.

With a feeling of constriction in her throat and her heart beating suffocatingly, she jumped out of bed and ran to the kitchen. Papa was sitting at the table with his head in his hands.

'Papa,' she called softly.

He looked up. His face was haggard and his cheeks moist with tears.

Icy fingers of fear clutched at her heart and her knees began to shake.

'Is it the baby?' she asked, fearfully.

Papa cleared his throat and slowly shook his head. 'No, the baby is fine,' he replied. Reaching out, he took her hands in his. 'It's your Mama.' His voice wavered and faded away.

'Mama!' she gasped, a cold chill running up her spine.

'Yes, my child. She was too weak and it was a difficult birth.'

Kate's mouth dried and it felt as if her vocal cords were glued together. The grip of his hands tightened.

'What do you mean, Papa?' She gasped, almost shouting as the panic welled up in her.

Papa looked past her and his eyes filled with tears. 'She's gone.'

Instinctively, Kate understood. 'You mean she's dead, Papa?'

He nodded, unable to speak.

For a moment her mind went completely blank with shock. Fate can play a cruel trick that no one can prepare you for. She stood staring at Papa disbelievingly and then she turned and ran to her room. Throwing herself on the bed she cried as if her heart was breaking. Beautiful kind Mama! She'll never see her again, never speak to her,

She heard Papa call as he sat down at the bottom of her bed. 'Please help me,' he said, softly. 'I need you to look after the baby.'

Deep gasping sobs shook her body. When she felt she could no longer cry she lifted her head and looked dejectedly at Papa. He ran a nervous hand through his hair. Suddenly she felt protective towards him and a surge of pity flooded over her. Trying to master her grief, she rose to her feet. 'Poor Papa,' she sighed, drying her eyes. 'Have they taken Mama away?'

'No,' Papa replied. 'Come with me.'

Gently he took her hand and led her into the room. It was in darkness. A single candle flickered fitfully in its holder on the table. Mama was lying on the bed. It looked as if she was sleeping peacefully. There was a soft smile on her lips. The next few minutes were to remain indelibly imprinted into Kate's memory. She pressed Papa's hand. 'She's beautiful, Papa,' she whispered.

He nodded and tears poured down his cheeks. 'She will always be with me,' he choked, and laid his hand on his heart, 'here.'

Kate leaned over the bed and kissed Mama's forehead. She was cold, so cold. 'Goodbye, Mama,' she whispered. 'I promise to look after the baby and Papa.' The words came out automatically.

Suddenly she heard a small noise and on looking down beside the bed she saw the basket. There, all pink and freshly washed, was the baby.

'It's a girl. We've called her Maggie,' Papa said, flatly.

Kate gazed at the baby in wonder and then picked her up very carefully, holding her tightly in her arms. 'She's lovely,' Kate whispered.

'Aunt Clara has offered to look after you and Maggie but I know Mama would be happier if we stayed together as a family. What do you think?' Papa looked at her intently before adding, 'I know you're only eleven and a half years old, but you'll be a big help in bringing up Maggie.'

'We must stay together,' Kate insisted, trying to hold back a fit of sobbing that threatened to engulf her. 'No time for tears,' she hissed.

Mama was buried the following day in the family burial ground not far from the big house.

When Kate returned after the funeral she went to her room and sat on the bed. She whispered, 'Grief is horrible. It attaches itself to your soul and leaves you feeling numb.' The weight of her misery pressed down on her as the awful truth came upon her that nothing was ever going to be the same again without Mama and just when things were going well....

Maggie began to whimper.

CHAPTER FIVE

A few days after the funeral Kate sat on the verandah at the front of the house, deep in thought. Aunt Clara had arranged with one of the black women who had recently had a baby, to come and feed Maggie every four hours. After three months Maggie would go on to the bottle. She was asleep tied securely with a blanket to Mintjie's back, as she did her work. Kate didn't know how she would have managed without Mintjie. She missed Mama terribly. Every now and again she thought she heard Mama calling and would turn around eagerly, only to find no one there.

She swallowed hard when she saw Uncle Hendrik making his way towards her. As he drew near she noticed the sorror in his eyes which mirrowed her own sense of loss and despair. Kate put her hand to her mouth to check the sob that welled up in her throat.

'My little angel,' Uncle Hendrik whispered, 'I'm so sorry, very sorry. How's the baby?'

'She's well, thank you,' Kate replied, her voice flat and lifeless.

He put his hand gently under her chin and lifted her head. 'You must now become a woman and care for her as your mama would have done.' Pausing, he opened his mouth as if to say something, changed his mind, and walked away, his shoulders sagging dejectedly.

That evening, after Maggie had had her last feed, Kate put her in her cot and patted her gently for a short while until she was asleep. She usually slept well during the night. Occasionally, she would wake up and Kate would give her some water after which she fell asleep until morning.

Kate went to the kitchen, made Papa something to eat, then went to bed. She had a yearning to see Mama again and felt too depressed to be able to speak even to Papa. The pain inside her made her feel numb. She was suddenly angry. 'Why did Mama have to die?' She cried, her eyes blurring with tears. She lay back on the bed and couldn't stop the tears from pouring down her face. Her mind went back to those carefree days in the Cape and there came over her an overwhelming longing to hear Mama's voice and see her smile. Finally, exhaustion dropped a certain over her despair and she drifted into a fitful sleep. She awoke later to find the room lit up and she clearly saw Mama, candle in hand, standing at the foot of the bed. Her eyes were cloaked with sadness. Kate sat up with a jerk, her head dizzy with sleep. Wiping her eyes with the back of her hand, she blinked in disbelief. 'Mama!' she cried, 'You've come back!'

Mama shook her head. 'No, dear Kate. I've come to ask you to stop grieving for me. Every time you cry your tears put out my candle and I cannot find my way to my loved ones who are waiting for me.' Suddenly she was gone.

Bewildered, Kate stared into the blackness. Then the message of her visit dawned on her. 'I won't cry anymore, Mama,' she whispered. 'There'll be no more tears.' From that moment on her sadness gradually left her.

Four years passed. The farm flourished and so did Maggie. On the first Saturday in every month Uncle Hendrik would load up the horse and cart with vegetables and biltong and Aunt Clara's wares such as soap, candles, crocheted doileys, bottled fruit and preserve, and go to the market in Bloemfontein. It was a two hour journey by horse and cart and he would leave at four in the morning and return at six in the evening. Occasionally Kate accompanied him on the long journey and she enjoyed the hustle and bustle of the market.

Each evening, after the days work was over and Maggie was tucked into bed, Papa and Kate sat in the kitchen and talked until it was time to retire.

'Uncle Hendrik has been like a father to me,' said Papa one evening. 'I don't know how we would have managed after losing Mama, without his and Aunt Clara's help.' Worry lines were etched deep across his forehead and round his eyes.

'You've also helped Uncle Hendrik,' Kate reminded him.

'I know. He has told me that on many occasions.' He looked sad for a moment and then his face lit up. 'Uncle Hendrik told me that if anything happened to him the farm is mine.'

Kate looked intently at Papa and saw that he was beaming with enthusiasm. She was suddenly very afraid and cried out, 'Papa! I'm happy for your sake, but I do hope nothing happens to Uncle Hendrik.'

Sensing Kate's anxiety, Papa laughed to reassure her. 'I share your thoughts,' he replied, 'but he's as strong as an ox so don't worry.'

His remark cheered Kate up and the rest of the evening he told her stories of when he was a boy. He had her laughing almost hysterically at all the pranks he used to get up to. It was good to see him so light hearted.

During the long hot summer months the heat was unbearable and at noon after the midday meal, Maggie and Kate would lie down for a couple of hours. It was still very hot one afternoon when Kate and Maggie donned their long bonnet-shaped caps, made of material that fell behind and across their shoulders, and walked to the collection of huts. When they visited Mintjie and her family Langbeen had to be chased home for he always picked a fight with the dogs at the huts and more often than not, he came off second best.

'Langbeen home!' Kate shouted, as he tried to follow.

'Langbeen go!'screamed Maggie. 'Other dogs hurt you.' She looked up at Kate and smiled.

Langbeen dropped his head sadly and walked back with his tail between his legs.

Life on the farm had been particularly good for Maggie. She had rosy cheeks and dark, curly hair that protruded from below the brim of her bonnet. Her eyes were a sparkling blue.

When they reached the circle of huts, surrounded by a hedge of thorn bushes, the small children stopped their play and ran to meet them. They invited Maggie to join them and she readily agreed. Some young women were stamping corn into meal. To lighten their task they sang in tune with the stamping, their sticks rising and falling in unison. Kate went to find Mintjie and have a drink of calabash milk. She had acquired the taste of the sour milk since living on the farm. Mintjie was in her hut. Laughing. Kate ran to her. 'What's up, Mintjie?' she asked.

Her eyes were dancing with merriment. 'It's Lena. She's jealous of me and always tries to get me into trouble with the Chief, our husband. Today she dropped the Chief's food to the ground.' She put her hands to her mouth chuckling at the thought. 'The Chief was very angry and came to my hut to share my food.'

'You don't like her, do you Mintjie?' Kate asked, looking at her intently.

'No. She causes too much trouble for everyone.'

Kate didn't trust Lena and feared for Mintjie. There was no knowing what she would hatch up to get even with her. Mintjie's joy was so infectious that Kate dismissed her gloomy thoughts and joined in her laughter.

Smiling, she handed Kate a calabash. After she had drunk her fill of thick milk, which she found soothing and refreshing, she thanked her and handed it back. They talked for a while and later Kate went to find Maggie.

That evening, after Kate had told Maggie a story and tucked her into bed, she sat in the kitchen with Papa.

'Can I make you some cocoa, Papa?' she asked.

'Yes, please, Kate. While you are making it I have some news to tell you.'

'What news, Papa,' she asked, curious.

'Someone has told Uncle Hendrik about a seed sewing machine that was recently imported into the Cape. From what he has been told it's a very primitive machine but,' he paused, 'it works and could be of tremdous help to us. He has made enquiries in Bloemfontein but none of the merchants there seem to be interested in getting supplies of this machine. It looks as though farmers are very conservative about such things. Uncle Hendrik has asked me to go to the Cape to see what I can find out.'

Kate caught her breath. 'When Papa?'

'I'll be leaving early tomorrow morning and I hope to be back within ten days. Sooner if I can. Maybe I'll bring back a surprise.' He smiled.

He didn't often smile and Kate was happy to see he was excited about the forthcoming trip. Uncle Hendrik was letting Papa do more of the running of the large farm these days. He said it was time he started to slow down as he was getting old. Kate always noticed a mischievous glint in his eyes when he told them this. Aunt Clara would grunt in disbelief. 'You give up work,' she scoffed, 'that day I want to see.'

While Papa was drinking his cocoa he said he would find time to call on the van Soelens.

'Oh, Papa,' Kate said excitedly, 'Could I write Poppie a letter?'

He laughed. 'Of course.'

Kate took some writing paper from a drawer in the kitchen cupboard and sat down at the table. 'I often long to see her, Papa,' she told him and sighed.

He looked at her thoughtfully and then said, 'One of these days I'll take you and Maggie to the Cape.'

'You will?' Kate was overjoyed and ran and hugged him. She quickly wrote a short note to Poppie telling her about Mama, Maggie and life on the farm and that one day they were sure to meet again and how much she looked forward to that day.

Rising early the next morning she packed some food for Papa to take on the long train journey. After kissing him goodbye he walked over to Uncle Hendrik who was taking him to the station. For some reason Kate couldn't define, as she watched his departing figure, she had an overwhelming feeling of love for him and for some reason a flicker of fear also came over her. She clicked her tongue angrily.

It was later that afternoon when Uncle Hendrik, his face ashen, came slowly into the kitchen.

'What's wrong, Uncle Hendrik?' she cried. A sick sensation came into her stomach.

'Kate,' he began.

Kate could feel the despair in his voice and tremors of fear ran up and down her spine. 'Papa's dead!' she exclaimned in anguish.

Uncle Hendrik took a sharp intake of breath and stared at her incredulously before nodding. 'How did you know?' he gasped.

'I don't know. I just did,' she heard herself reply. 'What happened?'

'There was a train accident just outside Bloemfontein station.'

Kate was too stunned to cry.

'I'm sorry, Kate. It should have been me.' His eyes filled with pain. 'You and Maggie must come and live with us now. We will love you as if you were our own.'

Kate stared at him uncomprehendingly and suddenly became afraid. When was it going to stop? Was life only about losing the things we love the most?

CHAPTER SIX

After Papa's death, the next few weeks slipped by in a haze of unreality. There was no word for what Kate was feeling. Sad didn't even come close. The day to day living had little or no impact on her. She felt empty inside. First Mama and now Papa. Aunt Clara had packed all their belongings and moved them to the big house.

For days her eyes were red-rimmed and Uncle Hendrik's face was masked with sadness. He spent nearly all the daylight hours in the lands, returning only for meals and to sleep.

At night Kate's eyes burned with unwashed tears. She wanted to cry to soften the pain in her chest but she couldn't. She knew Aunt Clara was concerned about her for she would often say, 'Kate, my child, death is only an extension of life. I know your grief is deep but sometimes to cry can be a relief.' She would then shake her head sadly and add, 'Sadness has a season and will pass.'

Kate would nod, but without conviction. Visions of Mama's visit would come into her mind. What if tears put out the candle Papa was carrying? It had to burn brightly so that he could find Mama.

Maggie was bewildered for she couldn't understand what had happened to Papa. Whenever she asked for him, Aunt Clara would tell her he had gone to live with Mama, leaving her more confused than before.

Moving to the big house was beneficial to Kate because her home was too full of poignant memories. Many months were to pass before she ventured into the old homestead. Often in the late afternoons, as she walked past, she would glance subconsciously at the verandah expecting to see Mama and Papa sitting there, as they often did, watching the setting of the sun.

One night she couldn't sleep and lay listening to Maggie's steady breathing. She had an overwhelming desire to be with Uncle Hendrik and Aunt Clara. With a heavy heart she climbed out of bed and made her way to the dining room. She heard Uncle Hendrik talking. They were discussing her.

'What can we do for her, Clara?' he asked.

'There's nothing we can do,' replied Aunt Clara. 'As much as we love her she's got to fight her grief all by herself.

Before she knew what was happening, she threw herself into Aunt Clara's arms, and sobbed uncontrollably.

'Let the tears come,' Aunt Clara whispered. 'You mustn't try to hold back your grief.'

When her sobbing had ceased, Aunt Clara led her back to bed. From sheer exhaustion she fell into a deep sleep. The following day, for the first time in many months, she didn't wake up before dawn with a heavy heart.

The months slipped by and winter was upon them. The trees around the house and the fruit trees in the orchard, had shed their leaves. It was late one afternoon in early June when, after one of Uncle Hendrik's monthly visit to the market place in Bloemfontein, he came into the living room where Maggie, Aunt Clara and Kate were sitting sewing. Maggie had been given some material and a needle and thread and was trying to emulate Kate and Aunt Clara.

'Clara!' Uncle Henry called, chuckling. 'Stoffel is at a conference in Bloemfontein. He and Klaas came to see me at the market and I've invited them to come for lunch tomorrow.'

Aunt Clara's face lit up. 'Is Greta with him?'

'No! She thought about coming but as Stoffel would be at the conference all day she decided to stay at home.'

Kate looked from one to the other.

'You remember Klaas, Kate,' chuckled Uncle Hendrik.

Kate giggled for she remembered Klaas only too well. He worked on the railways and Uncle Hendrik had introduced him to her at the market. He was Aunt Clara's cousin, a funny old man with a busy beard and no teeth. His clothes looked as if they needed a wash, but he didn't seem to care. The farmers knew him well and teased him unmercifully. He would merely laugh and shrug his shoulders. Uncle Hendrik said he needed a wife to look after him.

'Stoffel is very high up in the government,' explained Uncle Hendrik. 'He married Aunt Clara's cousin, Greta., Klaas' sister. They live in Pretoria and have seven children.' He stopped and with his eyes twinkling, added, 'We have two.'

He picked up Maggie and held her high above his head before lowering her and kissing her cheek.

Maggie screamed with delight. 'More! More!' she shouted.

Uncle Henry duly obliged.

'It would have been nice to see Greta again,' mused Aunt Clara, 'we were good friends and I haven't seen her for many years.'

Klaas and Stoffel arrived shortly before lunch the next day. They arrived in a horse drawn cart, Klaas at the reigns. Kate gasped when she saw him. She hardly recognised him. His beard was trimmed and his hair had been washed, combed and smoothed down with a sweet smelling oil. His clothes were pressed and spotlessly clean. The whole affect was however spoiled because he was wearing old and very dirty veldschoens. Stoffel was short and fat. The small amount of hair on his almost bald head was as ginger as his beard. He had a round, cherubic face and Kate took an instant liking to him.

After greeting Stoffel, Aunt Clara looked admiringly at Klaas.

'Klaas!' she exclaimed, 'You look good! The world must be treating you well.'

Before he could reply,' she added, 'Come, both of you sit at the table. Lunch will soon be ready.'

Klaas smiled, revealing pink toothless gums, and took a seat next to Uncle Hendrik. 'I must do something now and again to try to look nice,' he said.

Everyone laughed, Klaas louder than anyone else.

Lena brought in the food. They bowed their heads and Uncle Hendrik asked the blessing. After they had eaten, the men went to the front room, called the voorkamer, and Aunt Clara and Kate helped Lena to clear the table. Then Aunt Clara left Kate and Lena to do the washing up. Mintjie came and took Maggie to the huts to play with the children. When Kate had finished helping Lena, she went to look for Aunt Clara and found her crocheting in the front room.

Stoffel, pipe in hand, was talking softly to Uncle Hendrik and Klaas, near the fireplace. He would point the stem of his pipe to whoever he was speaking to.

'I'm telling you things are not going well in the Transvaal. In Government circles rumoirs are that war is inevitable. President Kruger is not happy with the 'Uitlanders' and the British seem to be spoiling for a fight.'

Uncle Hendrik looked concerned. 'I've heard talk among the farmers at the Bloemfontein market. My father was one of the first to take up land here. If war comes I must fight.'

Kate heard Aunt Clara draw in her breath and froze.

'There was a big meeting in Bloemfontein last month, Hendrik,' said Klaas. 'I was working on the station when President Kruger's train came in. There were the Vierkleur flags of the Transvaal on either side of the cow-catcher and the Orange Free State flag on the front of the boiler. It was an impressive sight.'

Stoffel nodded. 'President Steyn organised the meeting. It was between President Kruger and Lord Milner, the British representative. He thought a conference would bring about a peace settlement.' He thoughtfully puffed on his pipe and blew smoke towards the ceiling.

'Yes, Hendrik. After the conference I spoke to Jan Smuts, Kruger's State Attorney. Now there's a shrewd and brilliant man for you. He said he was suspicious of Milner because he was sly and a man to watch.'

'If the Transvaal goes to war will the Free State help them?' asked Klaas.

'Klaas! Do you think the Boers in the Free State will leave their brothers in the Transvaal to fight alone!' exclaimed Uncle Hendrik.

'Let's hope it doesn't come to war,' interjected Stoffel. 'President Steyn is sure that a peaceful settlement can still be found.

Peaceful settlement! War! What could it all mean? Kate looked at Aunt Clara. There was a worried frown on her face.

Later, after coffee together with Aunt Clara's fresh bread and jam, they left.

As the days passed, Kate came to realise that things were happening that she didn't understand. Many men called on Uncle Hendrik and there were frequent meetings in the house. On several occasions she heard it said that the 'Uitlanders' were looking for trouble and wanted to take over the country.

Late one afternoon Kate was in the living room with Aunt Clara when once again she heard the sound of raised voices coming from the front room.

'Aunt Clara, I'm frightened,' she whispered, 'What is it all about?'

Aunt Clara sighed. 'I don't exactly know what's going on. It seems as though there's some problem in the Transvaal Republic which will also affect the Free State. When gold was first discovered in the Transvaal, many, many people came from all over the world to make their fortune. President Kruger is not happy to have so many 'uitlanders' as they are called. He allows them to mine for gold, but he doesn't want them to have any say in the running of the country. This they want to do as they feel they have a right to vote in the land where they live and work. The Boers fear they will eventually take the land from them.'

'Does this mean there'll be a war?' Kate asked, her voice a mere whisper.

'I believe the Boers will fight for their land, Kate.'

Kate couldn't comprehend what was happening. All she knew was that war was something to fear, for many people could die.

A short while later the men left and Uncle Hendrik came into the room looking grave. 'Where's Maggie?' he asked.

'Mintjie's putting her to bed,' replied Aunt Clara and then added, 'Something wrong?'

'Yes. I must talk to you and Kate. Maggie is too small to understand and I don't want to frighten her.'

Kate's heart began to race. What now, she thought? They had overcome the shock of Papa's death and their lives had settled into a quiet routine and now there was all this talk of war.

'As you know,' Uncle Hendrik began, 'Something's going on in the land. The British and the Boers will soon be at war.'

'Must you go, my husband?' broke in Aunt Clara, fearfully.

Kate remained silent and studied Uncle Hendrik closely. His brow was deeply furrowed and he was staring at his hands.

'I've always been a man of peace,' he said.

Aunt Clara blurted, 'Hendrik, you are fifty five years old. Why must you go to war? Leave it to the younger men.'

A sense of utter despair swept over Kate. It was as though, once again, the world around her was crumbling.

'Clara, every able-bodied man and boy between the ages of fourteen and seventy will be needed and I'm strong and healthy. How can you expect me to stay away and let the others do the fighting?'

They sat for a while in silence, each with their own thoughts. At last Aunt Clara said, almost in a whisper, 'I realised only too well there was a threat of war, but I kept on hoping it would pass.'

Uncle Hendrik nodded. 'I didn't say anything to you before because I'd hoped that common sense would prevail.' He turned and looked at them. 'I'll fight to protect my wife and children. I've been told to be ready because at any time I'll have to go on commando. Kate, Aunt Clara will need you as she will have the responsibility of looking after the farm. You'll have to be brave.'

She smiled at him. She reached out and touched Uncle Hendrik and Aunt Clara on the arm. 'I know we'll come through,' she told them.

Uncle Hendrik nodded and smiled. 'That's the way to talk, Kate. No matter what happens, have that always in mind.'

From that moment onwards Aunt Clara spent each day with Uncle Hendrik in the lands to learn the running of the farm and Kate, after helping Maggie with her lessons, worked in the house. Aunt Clara seemed to age overnight. Her hair became greyer and a worried expression seldom left her face.

Things between Lena and Mintjie came to a head when they had a fight. Lena accused Mintjie of trying to steal her job and wouldn't allow her into the kitchen. Mintjie ignored her but as she entered the kitchen one morning, Lena, like a ferocious animal, sprang at her and threw her to the ground.

Mintjie's cries were heard by Uncle Hendrik and Aunt Clara and they came rushing to her rescue. Much to Kate's relief, Aunt Clara told Lena she had to go. Mintjie feared going back to the huts so Uncle Hendrik went to see the Chief and told him to warn Lena that if she harmed Mintjie he would have her removed from the farm. There was no further trouble.

One night three weeks later, Kate was awakened by the sound of voices. At first she couldn't hear what was being said but gradually the voices became louder. She climbed out of bed and looked out of the window. The stars were twinkling brightly against the moonlit sky.

As her eyes grew accustomed to the subdued light she could make out a crowd of men on horseback near the fence. With beating heart she hurried from the room and found Uncle Hendrik and Aunt Clara in the kitchen.

Uncle Hendrik was dressed in his Sunday clothes. Across his chest was a bandolier of ammunition. He was holding a rifle. Aunt Clara handed him a parcel of food.

Kate felt a sick sensation in her stomach. This is it. War!

'Go well, Hendrik,' said Aunt Clara, 'May God spare you.'

Kate ran into Uncle Hendrik's arms. He hugged her and kissed the top of her head. 'Be brave, little one,' he said, hoarsely, adding, 'God help us and our people.'

After kissing Aunt Clara goodbye he turned and walked out of the kitchen. Aunt Clara took the lamp from the table and together they followed him on to the verandah. He walked down the steps and joined the others. Each man had a rifle strung over his shoulders and a bandolier.

'Goodbye!' they called.

'Goodbye!' responded Aunt Clara, flatly.

Uncle Hendrik mounted his horse and with a clatter of hooves, the party rode off into the night.

They stood there motionless, listening to the sound of the horses as they faded into the distance, wondering what the unknown tomorrows held for them.

CHAPTER SEVEN

Immediately after the departure of Uncle Hendrik, Aunt Clara began working for long hours in the lands.

So much happened in the months that followed. Life took on a new momentum. Mintije and Kate, with a little help from Maggie, made biltong from the carcasses of buck brought to them from the young black men on the farm. They also cooked all the meals, kept the house clean, made butter, soap and candles. There was little time for play and even less time to worry. At night, exhausted from their labours, they retired early to bed. In spite of the absence of Uncle Hendrik and even in all the uncertainty of the war, Kate felt contented with her lot. Maggie was a great delight to her. She grew tall and strong and her gracious nature endeared her to everyone.

Kate's busy days didn't give her a chance to dwell on what the future had in store for them.

During the months that followed a steady stream of Boers, mostly ragged and war weary, called at the farm for food and a place to rest for a few hours. Now and again Boers passed by the farm on their way to join de Wet's guerillas. News of his occupation of the Waterworks at Sannaspos, east of Bloemfontein, boosted morale to such an extent that more and more Boers joined him. Even though the Transvaal fell to the British, the Free Staters were not prepared to give up without a struggle.

To Kate there was something very moving about the courage of those Boers. Aunt Clara welcomed them gladly for she felt she was helping the Boer cause. She enquired of each caller if they knew the whereabouts of Uncle Hendrik, but no one had seen or heard of him. They did however, learn that the war was not going well for the Boers. Although the British had suffered a severe reverse at Magersfontein, General Cronje and his commando of about four thousand men had been forced to surrender to Field Marshall Lord Roberts at Pardeberg on February 27, 1900. Some of the Boers who came to the farm were scathing in their critism of Cronje.

'We Boers,' one of them said, 'mustn't try to fight pitch battles with these people. Mobility is our secret weapon. Cronje couldn't understand this and there he sat, in his laager of heavily loaded oxwagons, as the British closed in on them.'

Even though Kate nursed the fear that they may become victims of the war, she never lost faith in a Boer victory.

Gradually the visits of the commandos ceased and for several weeks they were left in complete ignorance as to how the war was progressing. Furthermore, their lack of contact with the outside world was aggrevated by the fact that they never went into Bloemfontein, neither did they see their neighbours because their menfolk had also gone off to the war and they were too fully occupied with the running of their farms.

One afternoon, Kate took Maggie to the huts to play with the children. After leaving her there she strode up a small koppie on the far side of the huts and sat in the shade of an umbrella-shaped thorn tree. Resting her back against the rough trunk, she lazily stared at the vastness of the veld and drifted along on a sea of fantasy.

She imagined herself once again in the Cape talking to Poppie. She wondered how she was and if she too was affected by the war?

Overhead was a cloudless blue sky. Everything about her was so peaceful and she closed her eyes dreamily. She sat up with a start when, with a rush of wings, a guinea fowl rose noisily from a tuft of grass near to where she was sitting. She watched it scamper off into the veld. It was then she noticed a cloud of dust smudging the haze that blurred the horizon into the sky. She could make out a long line of uniformed horsemen.

She gasped in horror. They had to be the English soldiers, the dreaded Khakis! Trembling, she ran down the kopje as fast as she could, almost falling headlong into a thorny bush on the way down. Steadying herself, she ran to the huts and grabbed a surprised and protesting Maggie.

'Not so fast,' she pleaded.

But Kate ignored her pleas and was relieved to find Aunt Clara in the kitchen when they arrived. 'I saw a line of British soldiers,' she told her, out of breath.

Aunt Clara's eyes widened. 'If they're so close things can't be well for the Boers,' she whispered. 'Are they coming this way?'

She thought for a moment. 'They seemed to be heading in the direction of Bloemfontein.'

'Mmmmh,' muttered Aunt Clara, frowning. 'That's bad.!'

The following morning Kate awoke as dawn was breaking over the veld. She couldn't dispel the uneasy feeling that had crept over her since seeing the Khakis. Instinct warned her that great danger was to come.

She washed and dressed and went into the kitchen. Maggie and Aunt Clara were still sleeping. Kate opened the back door and walked on to the verandah. She stood for several minutes watching the sun climbing slowly over the horizon. To watch the dawn was a wonderful experience. The stars merged into a greyness and gradually the sky became splashed with orange and yellow as the sun rose higher and higher and the country began to lighten. Birds twittered as they searched for insects and she could hear the mournful piping of guinea-fowl as she watched the transformation of night into day.

Brakkies and Langbeen ran up to her wagging their tails. It semed as if every portion of their bodies were wriggling. She smiled as she patted them. Langbeen gave her a quick lick on her face. She screwed up her nose as she felt his warm, wet tongue and raised her hand to shield herself from another lick.

Suddenly Brakkies stiffened, his ears erect. She thought she heard the sound of horses. Brakkies disappeared around the side of the house, followed by Langbeen. She hastened after them. On reaching the front garden she saw a group of horsemen some distance away and a feeling of unease came over her.

The morning was crisp and cool and the scent of the roses on the fence filled the air. The horsemen came nearer and Kate almost froze to the spot. Khakis! She ran back into the house. By this time Aunt Clara and Maggie were up and in the kitchen.

'The Khakis are coming,' she blurted.

Aunt Clara said nothing, but her face paled. Maggie stared at Kate with frightend eyes.

They walked on to the verandah. Ten minutes later some British soldiers rode up to the farm. Kate couldn't help noticing how well dressed they were. Not like the Boers, she thought.

When they drew up to where they were standing a young officer, looking uncomfortable, said, 'Sorry, Mam, but we've been told to confiscate all your livestock and fodder.'

Aunt Clara started to protest but the officer held up his hand. 'Please don't make it hard for us, Mam, I don't want anyone to get hurt. We are only carrying out orders.'

Aunt Clara sighed and shook her head. A surge of anger rushed over Kate. Doubling her fists she was sorely tempted to lash out at the officer, but she knew their position was hopeless so remained silent. Instead, she clenched her fists until her nails were digging into the palms of her hands.

The officer turned and walked to his men who were gathered near the coach house, shouting orders as he went. A few minutes later one of the soldiers brought the two horses out of the stable.

Aunt Clara took Kate's and Maggie's hand and led them into the front room. 'Come, my children, we don't have to watch such things,' she said.

That evening, after Maggie had been put to bed, Aunt Clara said to Kate, 'The Khakis must be worried about the course of the war so they are trying to punish the Boers by taking their livestock, which is our wealth. We must do some hiding.'

Kate looked at her curiously. 'What must we hide?' she asked.

'My bottled fruit jam, biltong, candles and whatever else we can. I fear things are going to get worse before they improve.'

'Where can we hide these things?' Kate wanted to know.

'Mintjie can take Maggie to the huts to play with the children in the afternoons and we'll do some digging, but only you and I must know the whereabouts.'

During the next few afternoons Aunt Clara and Kate dug a long, deep trench in the coach house. The ground was hard and the work tiring. When they had finished they placed bottles of fruit, jam and preserve, soap, candles and biltong, in the trench. Aunt Clara also put a purse full of coins into it. Placing animal skins over the horde, they replaced the earth and, after scattering straw over the soft sand, stamped it down well with their feet.

'Good!' Aunt Clara exclaimed, satisfied, 'There's enough food to last us for a long time should we need it.'

Kate often awoke during the night not knowing what had disturbed her. Listening intently she would only hear the familiar night sounds, like the howl of a jackal or the ominous hoot of an owl. But she couldn't shake off the fear that gripped her.

Oom Hendrik arrived unexpectedly one morning. It was a day for rejoicing. All the labourers cheered when they saw him. Mintjie clapped her hands and smiled. 'I'm happy you safe, Master,' she said.

'Thank you, Mintjie,' Oom Hendrik replied. 'I'm happy to be back even for a short while.'

That evening, after we had eaten, we remained sitting at the table. Oom Hendrik lit his pipe and drew on it contentently. Since his arrival he had been quiet as if he had something weighing on his mind. 'Clara,' he began.

Aunt Clara looked at him guardedly.

'Bloemfontein has fallen to the British.'

Aunt Clara interrupted. 'A few days ago Kate saw a lot of Khakis riding in the direction of Bloemfontein.'

Uncle Hendrik nodded. 'Yes, Bloemfontein surrended without any resistance, but all is not lost.

'When did they surrender?' Aunt Clara asked.

'On the 13th March.'

'Does that mean the war is over?' Aunt Clara could not conceal the relief in her voice.

'No, Clara, Christiaan de Wet, the Chief Commander of the Free State, has only given us a few days leave. There's still too much at stake for us to give up now.'

Kate lookd at him sadly. When will this all end?

Maggie began to cry sensing something was wrong.

Uncle Hendrik picked her up and put her on his knee. He soon had her laughing.

'No more talk of war until the little one is in bed,' he said firmly.

Later, Kate put Maggie to bed. Her head had hardly touched the pillow when she was asleep. Returning to the room she found Uncle Hendrik and Aunt Clara deep in conversation.

'Come, Kate,' called Aunt Clara. 'You must also know what is going on.' Sighing, she added, 'It's hard to believe you are already sixteen years old. Tell Kate some of your experiences, Hendrik. I'm sure she'll be interested.'

He looked at Kate and chuckled. 'If it wasn't so serious it could be funny,' he said. 'Coming home I had to play hide and seek with the Khakis. They were everywhere, like flies in mid-summer.'

Kate smiled and nodded. 'Where have you been all these months, Uncle Hendrik.'

He sighed. 'Life has been hard in the veld. When we left here we rode for hours and joined up with the Transvaal Boers. We tried to grab a few hours rest in the early morning. There were no tents and it was cold, also it began to rain. Our commandant made us lie in long grass on our rifles to protect them. All we had to cover ourselves with were small pieces of canvas. We didn't even have macintoshes! But we were tired and slept for two hours. When we woke up we were drenched to the skin.'

'Did you get sick, Hendrik?' Aunt Clara asked, concerned.

'No. Funny enough not one of us even caught a cold. The sun came out and with the breeze, dried out our clothing. Later that day we came upon some Boers with loaded oxwagons. There were about fifty Boers.' He laughed at the memory. They brought everything with them. Beds, mattresses, family and servants. That was General Cronje's downfall at Paardeberg. His men were so laden down by oxwagons they couldn't get away from the British.'

Aunt Clara nodded. 'Several of the Boers who called on us said the same thing.'

Uncle Hendrik continued, 'We left those Boers to their oxwagons and went on our way. Our orders were to head towards the Natal border. Several small groups of Boers joined us on the way bringing our numbers up to about one hundred. Three days later, it was about six in the evening, we came across about fifty Khakis cooking their supper near a stream. We charged down on them. I think it must have been the smell of the food, because we hadn't eaten all day. As soon as they saw us they raised their hands and surrendered.' He laughed. 'We made them remove their trousers and their boots and chased them off into the veld. They left their rifles, ammunition and horses behind. With the food they were cooking and the tins of bully beef on their supply wagon, we all had a feast that night. In case they returned we posted guards.' Chuckling, he added, 'No soldier would come looking for a fight without their trousers or boots.'

'The next morning we set out again armed with extra horses, ammunition and food. At midday we met up with a small party of Boers under Field-Cornet du Plessis who told Commandant Skeepers, our commando, that Commandant Christian de Wet was gathering a force together near Lindley, a few kilometers away, to reinforce the Free Staters on the western front, near Kimberley. We set off in all haste and joined up with Commandant de Wet that evening. We spent the next day resting our horses and early the following morning we set off as part of de Wet's commando.' He paused to relight his pipe.

'What was Commandant de Wet like?' Kate asked.

'Before we met up with him it was as though we were on a holiday, but once we set off towards Kimberley with de Wet, the holiday was over. It took us several days to get to our destination and during that time we only had four or five hours sleep every night. Woe betide any man who fell asleep on guard duty. De Wet would lay about him with his sjambok.'

Kate cried out, 'That's cruel!'

'Yes, I agree, but a man on guard is entrusted with the lives of his companions. After several days of hard riding we came close to the Riet River. I remember the day well. It was the seventeenth of February, my birthday. The next day a raiding party, led by de Wet, ambushed a convoy of wagons at Waterval Drift. Most of the three thousand oxen stampeded. There were about two hundred loaded wagons. Biscuits, jam, corned beef, tinned milk, bandages, medicines and so on were found on these wagons. That was the good news but the bad news was that even though we had been sent to join General Cronje, we were prevented from doing so because there were too many Khakis between them and us. De Wet was a brave man. On Sunday, February eighteenth, now you know how we Boers don't do anything on Sundays but read our Bible and rest, but this Sunday the British General, Lord Kitchener, attacked General Cronje and his men at Paardeberg. The English lost a lot of men. We heard the rumble of heavy guns. After a hasty meal we saddled up and rode off in the direction of the gunfire. The sun was bad. It shone in our eyes and burnt our faces. As we drew near, the gunfire grew more intense. We came to a rise and Commandant de Wet ordered us to dismount and rest our horses. He sent out a party of scouts to spy out the land. They came back and reported to de Wet that General Cronje's laager was almost surrounded by the British. We remounted and rode as fast as we could to a kopje near the river. We were three hundred Boers against thousands of Khakis.

'Danie Theron, a Boer scout, risked his life by stealing through the British lines to give Cronje a message from de Wet telling him that he would be coming to help them, but it means that he and his men would have to make their escape across the flooded Modder river. The British attacked us. We managed to hold the kopje for three days. Cronje and his men stubbornly refused to leave. Finally, he was forced to surrender. Over four thousand men were taken prisoner. Thirteen hundred of them Free Staters!'

Aunt Clara came in, 'I don't blame Cronje. Crossing a flooded river with loaded oxwagons could mean disaster.'

'We tried in vain to block the British advance, but their troops were too numerous and in the end we had to retreat. After that it was easy for the British to take Bloemfontein. Moral is at its lowest, but we can't give up yet.'

Aunt Clara clicked her tongue. 'Hendrik, do we still have a chance to win?'

'Not if we have loaded oxwagons. We can win if we fight as commandos, always on the move.'

Two days later Uncle Hendrik had a visitor. He was introduced by Uncle Hendrik as 'Chief Commandant de Wet of the Free State.

Kate stared at the man that Uncle Hendrik had spoken of with such reverence. He was short and stocky and had deep penetrating eyes. He wore a brown corduroy jacket and his trousers were tucked into knee length boots. He held a wide-brimmed hat in his hand.

Aunt Clara made them some coffee.

'Hendrik,' de Wet said between sips of coffee, 'I want you to come with me to visit the farmers in the district. I've heard many are refusing to fight. We must point out that all is not lost and that the war can still be won. If we lay down our arms the Brits will walk over us.'

Uncle Hendrik agreed and an hour later we watched, with heavy hearts, as they rode away.

One morning, about four months later, a feeling of uneasiness came over Kate as she busied herself with her chores. When she was about to sit down for lunch the dogs began barking excitedly and there was a loud knocking on the back door. They looked at each other fearfully. Aunt Clara rose from the table and walked cautiously to the door. 'Who is it?' she called.

'Sergeant Brown. Mounted Yeomanry, open the door.'

As Aunt Clara opened the door Kate saw, standing on the verandah, a group of about twenty soldiers. They were unshaven and their uniforms were dishevelled.

Kate ran to Maggie and clasped her protectively. Instinctively, she knew these men were bad, not like the well spoken, clean and almost apologetic men who had last visited them.

'Get out of the house,' ordered the Sergeant. His eyes were bloodshot with the bleary expression of a drunkard and he had a strange loping gait.

'This is our house,' Aunt Clara insisted, her face flushed with anger.

'Look, lady, I'm not here to argue with you. Get out, if you know what's good for you!'

'What kind of people are you to make war on innocent women and children?' Aunt Clara demanded.

'Innocent!' roared the ill mannered sergeant. 'No more talk. Get out!'

Knowing she was beaten, Aunt Clara shrugged. 'Can I collect a few things for the children?' she asked, almost pleading with him.

'Only what you can carry in two hands,' he spat out.

With heavy hearts they went to their room.

'Take a blanket and some warm clothes, Kate,' Aunt Clara whispered.

Kate gave Maggie a blanket to carry. She looked at her fearfully, her eyes large and her lips quivering. 'Where are we going?' she asked, a sob in her voice.

Unable to speak, Kate shook her head and hid her face in the clothing she was holding.

As they walked out of the room Kate saw the soldiers taking crochet cloths, plates and pictures off the walls, some were family photographs.

'We can get money for these things,'said one.

'Yes, load up that old wagon outside,' replied another.

Aunt Clara came from her room, blankets and clothing piled high in her arms. As she walked past one of the soldiers he snatched a blanket and threw it to the floor. 'Not so much, old woman,' he snapped.

The others burst out laughing.

Aunt Clara said nothing, but holding her head high, walked outside. Maggie and Kate followed. Once outside, they watched helplessly as the Khakis, scooping the dried mealies and pumpkins off the roofs of the outbuildings, and carrying them into the house.

Kate stared at them in disbelief and wondered why they were doing such a crazy thing? Then she noticed smoke billowing out of the front door of their old home and felt a sickening sensation in her stomach. The realisation came to her that they were going to destroy the home. They obviously had no pity in their hearts.

The black labourers had congregated some distance from the house and were looking wide-eyed. Mintjie hastened up to them. She was crying.

They were too shocked and numb to cry.

CHAPTER EIGHT

The sergeant appeared on the verandah. 'You're fortunate we don't take you with us to Bloemfontein,' he sneered, before walking back into the house.

'Come, we must go,' Tant Clara insisted, her voice strained and Kate saw she was close to tears. 'There's no reason for us to stay here. We must find a place where we will be safe until all the unpleasantness is over.'

'Where can we go?' Kate asked.

'To the kopje near the dam. There's a cave around there somewhere. I don't trust these Khakis. They may come back for us. We'll make a shelter in the veld and work out later what we can do.'

Mintjie walked with us as they made their way dejectedly across the veld to the kopje, carrying their few belongings. Kate wished with all her heart that they could be whisked away to the Cape by a magic geni. One thing was certain in life, she thought, just when everything was going well it was sure to go wrong.

A shot rang out, then another. Fire had burst out of the windows and doors of their home with a loud roaring. Volumes of smoke rolled overhead. They stopped and turned momentarily before continuing on their way. When they were almost at the foot of the kopje, they looked back again. Clouds of black smoke was still climbing into the sky.

'There goes our life's work,' choked Aunt Clara. 'Generations of my family have also gone up in smoke.

What upsets me the most, is the loss of the photographs. They chart our journey through life.'

Kate could feel the deep dispair in her voice. She swallowed the lump that came into her throat and her heart pounded as a surge of rage and hatred swept over her.

'You can stay with me,' invited Mintjie, looking first at Kate and then Aunt Clara.

'Thank you Mintjie, but I don't want the soldiers to burn your hut because you are helping us. We'll manage somehow.'

When they arrived at the koppie they found a rough shelter formed by two large boulders.

'This will do for a while,' said Aunt Clara. 'Let's gather some leaves and grass to put on the floor. It'll be softer than sleeping on the hard ground.'

They spent the rest of the afternoon preparing their shelter. When evening came Mintjie brought them three straw mats and a large pot of porridge.

'You're a good woman, Mintjie,' Aunt Clara said softly, her eyes brimming with tears.

Mintjie smiled self-conciously. 'You were always good to me, Madam,' she said.

That night it was cold in the shelter and they huddled close together for warmth. It took a long time to fall asleep as the screaming of the owls and bats together with the other wildlife, kept them awake. Also when the wind blew its mournful moaning made Kate shudder.

The next morning they walked back to the farm, or what was left of it. The roofs had collapsed and only the blackened walls remained. Even the outbuildings and the coach house had been razed to the ground. Aunt

Clara looked at the desolation through the tears that poured down her face unashamedly. Kate touched her arm gently. She wiped her eyes on her pinafore and inhaled deeply several times.

'We must not let this get us down, Kate,' she said angrily, through gritted teeth. 'Right will always triunph over might.' But Kate could see she was not entirely convinced.

They searched amongst the rubble and found a pot, a few buckled spoons, the blade of a knife and two pieces of scorched roof iron from the coach house.

'We'll need those,' Aunt Clara said, pointing to the iron. 'They'll protect us from the rain.'

Maggie found a chamber pot. They laughed. 'We'll need that if we are desperate during the night,' came in Aunt Clara. 'Too dangerous to go out into the darkness. Fortunately we do have the pit toilet we can use during the day or the long grass if we are too far away. We still have some porridge Mintjie brought us. We'll also look in the fields. Maybe there'll be left over mealies and potatoes.'

In a panic Kate asked, 'Where's Langbeen and Brakkies? I haven't seen them since we left.'

Before Aunt Clara could reply, Mintjie came hurrying around the corner proudly holding a plucked chicken. 'Mam!' she called. 'The Khakis couldn't catch all the chickens and they are running all over the veld.' She giggled.

'Where's Langbeen and Brakkies?' Maggie asked, tearfully.

Mintjie stared at us and, turning to Aunt Clara said, 'They're dead. The Khakis shot them. Imvane, the goatherd, buried them.'

It was then Kate remembered the two shots they heard as they walked away from the house. A sudden wave of revulsion flowed over her. 'I hate them!' she screamed. 'They are cruel and evil, killing poor old dogs.'

Maggie began to cry uncontrollably.

Aunt Clara placed her hand tenderly on Kate's shoulder and Kate burst into tears.

'In a way it's a good thing the dogs are not here anymore,' she told us. 'We would have trouble finding food for them and they could also give our hiding place away.' She bent down and cradled Maggie and Kate in her arms. 'Don't grieve, my children. Come, let's go back to our shelter. We must make a fire to cook our chicken.'

Smiling, Mintjie came in. 'I'll bring you another chicken tomorrow. I may find some eggs too.' She turned to leave.

'Mintjie, could you let us have some matches?' Aunt Clara asked, 'and maybe a candle?'

'Yes, Mam,' Mintje called over her shoulder.

By this time Maggie and Kate had stopped crying and were looking up at Aunt Clara expectantly.

'Roast chicken will taste better than porridge,' Kate said, suddenly light-hearted.

Aunt Clara chuckled. 'I quite agree. Let's go and prepare our feast.'

When they arrived at the shelter they placed one of the pieces of iron horizontally over the two rocks. The other piece they left lying near the entrance. Then, whilst Aunt Clara was building the fire, Maggie and Kate searched the koppie for pieces of brushwood which, together with large stones, they placed on the horizontal sheet of iron to anchor it. Their hideout was now well concealed.

'At night we'll cover the entrance with the other piece of iron,'Aunt Clara told them, adding, 'It will also keep out all the creepy crawlies.'

Kate shuddered, 'Meaning snakes and other wild life.'

When, in later years, Kate looked back on these long months of privation in the veld, she would realise that from the time they moved to their home on the kopje, they became so absorbed in the day-to-day problems of cooking their food, keeping themselves moderately clean, they had no time to bemoan their lot or to worry over the future. One week seemed to meld into another. Kate realised that when there was something to do, fear wears off and they find themselves too busy to worry.

The walls of the farm houses and outbuildings, standing stark and smoke blackened against the austere veld, were clearly visible from their shelter, grim reminders of the comfort and security they once had known. Nights spent huddled together on the hard ground was another matter. Sleep never came easily to Kate. She had too much time, both to recall the past and to contemplate, with forboding, whatever the future might hold in store for them. She spent many sleepless hours wondering whether the world was essentially evil? Other than Uncle Hendrik, Aunt Clara and the sweet innocent Maggie, she knew so few people.

What of those men in Khaki? Did they not have homes and families of their own? Why did they burn and plunder the farm with such relish? The young officer who had led the party that drove off their livestock had a kindly manner and said they were merely carrying out orders. He looked uncomfortable when he spoke. Soldiers were supposed to be brave. She clicked her tongue angrily when she remembered Aunt Clara telling her that a soldier had to obey orders or be shot!

Often when walking in the veld with Maggie, Kate would search the far distance for a lone figure who might be Uncle Hendrik returning from the war. On several occasions she noticed Aunt Clara doing the same and surmised that she may have been on the look-out for the Khakis. She never questioned her on this.

If only Uncle Hendrik would return. Perhaps they could then set about starting to rebuild the farm, or what was left of it. For the present, as Aunt Clara said soon after they had arrived, it was merely the case of staying alive until Uncle Hendrik returned and the war was over.

Aunt Clara had said this to her one evening as they were rekindling the fire. When she had spoken her voice trailed off and once again she searched the distant, empty horizon. As long as she still hoped for his return, that was all that mattered.

Every morning, before breakfast, they walked down to the dam that bordered the huts, to wash in the cool, clear water. Sometimes Mintjie would be able to let them have some home-made lye and they would strip themselves and bathe amongst the tall rushes that clustered along the bank. They had to be continually on their guard against the many dangers that could creep up on them. Wild animals roamed the veld and often the silence of the night was disturbed by the distant roar of a lion. Snakes too were a problem, especially during the summer months.

As the weeks went by the supply of chickens dwindled until finally they were forced to exist on porridge, potatoes, herbs and guinea fowl. There was plenty of fruit on the trees, but some of it was beginning to rot.

Maggie and Kate became adept at trapping guinea fowls in a box with one end held open with a stick to which was attached along piece of string. They would lie concealed behind a rock or bush holding the other end of the string. As an unwary fowl entered the box to inspect the porridge, Kate pulled the string. The door closed, the trap was sprung.

Smoke from the fire was a cause for concern. Their brazier was made from an old tin with the top cut off and holes punched in. It rested on two stones and they made the fire between the stones. When they first moved into the shelter the fire was lit just outside the entrance. On windless days a long column of smoke climbed high into the air. To reduce the smoke that could betray their whereabouts, Aunt Clara recited the fire close to an umbrella shaped tree so that the smoke filtered through the leaves and was less noticeable.

One afternoon, while Maggie was at the huts playing with the children, Kate went with Aunt Clara to inspect the floor of the coach house where she had buried their 'hidden treasure', as she had told Kate.

It was still intact.

As they walked back to the kopje they agreed that it would remain there undisturbed until they ran out of food.

'We will live off the land for as long as possible,' Aunt Clara said.

By now they had been living in the veld for many months. In spite of their frugal diet they were nonetheless in good health. Subconsciously, over the months, they developed the habit during the daylight hours, of watching the Khakis. On several occasions small parties of horsemen came into view as they rode across the veld. Some were Boer commandos, but more often than not the horsemen were the enemy.

Once a stray Boer came upon them on the kopje. He didn't know who had the biggest shock. It was early in the morning. As Aunt Clara removed the sheet of iron from the entrance of their shelter, they saw, sitting a few metres from them, a young man.

'My word!' exclaimed Aunt Clara, her gaze softening. 'It's a young Boer.'

He had black hair and a very bushy black beard. His clothes were torn and caked with dried mud. When he saw them his eyes nearly popped out of his head. 'What you doing here, living like hares?' he gasped.

'I'm Clara van Heerden, and these are my children, Kate and Maggie,' Aunt Clara explained. 'Our farm was plundered and burnt.'

Shaking his head he said sadly, 'This war is bad when women and children have to suffer. My name's Japie van Vuuren. I escaped when a patrol of Khakis suddenly came across a few of us making our way back to our commando after scouting out the land. They were as surprised as we were.' He laughed and stroked his beard. 'As there were more of them than there were of us, we scattered into the surrounding hills. They chased after us. I managed to escape, but became separated from the others.'

'Will you be able to find them again?' Kate asked.

He smiled. 'Yes. Just resting for a moment.' He looked at us thoughtfully before adding, 'You can be thankful the Khakis didn't take you to the camp in Bloemfontein. They've been herding the Boer women and children into this camp where they have to stay until the war is over. I've heard there's much suffering there. Many women and children have died.' He rose to his feet and mounted his horse. 'Have you seen any Khakis?' he asked.

Aunt Clara shook her head. 'Not for some time.'

Nodding, he waved and rode away.

Kate shuddered. So that was what the sergeant had meant when he said, 'You're lucky we don't take you with us to Bloemfontein.'

'We must be even more careful not to be seen by the Khakis,' said Aunt Clara. 'We don't want to be herded into camps like sheep.'

Early one morning in November, the year nineteen hundred and one, as the first light of dawn was breaking over the veld, Kate was awakened from a fitful sleep by the distant sound of galloping horses. For a moment she thought she might have imagined the sound. She quietly moved the sheet of iron to one side and crept out of the shelter. Climbing stealthily to the top of the kopje, she peered from behind a large boulder and could make out a long line of mounted Khakis coming slowly towards the kopje in extended order.

Bending low, she hastened back over the broken ground to the shelter. 'Wake up, Aunt Clara,' she whispered, urgently. 'The khakis are coming towards this kopje.'

CHAPTER NINE

Aunt Clara sat bolt upright, blinked, and stared myoptically about her. 'We must hide,' she whispered.

Kate nodded and gently placed her hand over Maggie's mouth. She woke with a start. 'Not a sound, Maggie,' Kate hissed. 'The Khakis are coming and we have to hide.'

Maggie rubbed her eyes and stood up. Quickly they bundled their few belongings into two blankets and hurried down the kopje towards the dam. As they did so they could clearly hear the sound of the horses and an occasional shout from the other side of the kopje. Reaching the safety of the willow trees that bodered the dam, they sank breathlessly to the ground.

Kate separated some of the branches that enshrouded them and looked up at the kopje. The long line of horsemen were clearly in sight on the top. Two metres below them was their hideout. Kate touched Aunt Clara's arm. 'Look!' she whispered, as she pointed to the dense thicket of trees and bushes next to them. 'It's much thicker in there. Maggie and I were here a few days ago when we were looking for guinea fowl.'

Aunt Clara nodded and picking up their bundles, Kate led her and Maggie into the dense thicket. They had to walk with one arm held out to stop the branches from scratching their faces and, bending low to avoid, as much as possible, the sharp thorns and twigs that tugged them. When they penetrated into what appeared to be the dense part of the thicket, they lay listening and waiting. Maggie snuggled up close beside Kate.

Looking at her expectantly, she whispered, 'We play hide and seek with the Khakis.'

Kate smiled and nodded, placing a finger over her lips. Over the months, Kate noticed how Maggie had not only come to accept, but even to enjoy, life in the veld.

By now the sun had risen clear of the horizon, but their place of concealment was so dense it remained encased in a muted darkness, yet they could make out quite clearly the sounds of the Khakis as they drew near.

Listening intently, Kate realised that the soldiers must have discovered their shelter, thus giving impetus to their search. There came to her the sound of someone moving noisily towards them through the thicket. They could hear his boots crunching over the ground. A loud shout followed, then voices raised in what she took to be an argument. This continued for a minute or so then, much to Kate's relief, the voices ceased. She listened to the sounds made by the men as they trampled amongst the willows. Gradually the sounds faded into the still morning air.

Aunt Clara looked at us, her eyes twinkling. 'Neither of you speak English, although you Kate have a smattering of the language, but you wouldn't have known what the Khakis were arguing about. The one who came closer to us was complaining about the branches and twigs that were scratching his face. Then he found one of Maggie's vests. We must have dropped it in our haste. The Khaki and his companion, after carefully examining the undergarment came to the conclusion that it was so threadbare it must have been thrown away.'

Kate smiled and replied, 'Just our luck they thought that.'

After waiting for some time they picked up their bundles and made their way out of the thicket. Once they had skirted the dam they came to the edge of the trees and looked anxiously up at the kopje. A group of about ten Khakis were waiting on their horses a hundred metres from their shelter. A figure detatched itself from amongst the group and ran down the kopje.

'Look, Aunt Clara!' Kate whispered, 'That's Lena.'

'Yes,' she replied, sadly, 'She's betrayed us. Now that the Khakis have discovered our hiding place they may come back to look for us. We'll have to find another shelter.'

Kate sighed and nodded.

Some time later the soldiers rode off. They waited until they couldn't see them anymore. Once out of the thicket, Kate shielded her eyes from the sun and looked about her. She saw a figure approaching. 'Here comes Mintjie!' she exclaimed, waving to her.

She drew near and a smile lit up her face. 'Oh, Mam, Kate, Maggie,' she cried, her eyes welling up with tears of relief. 'I'm glad you are safe. The Khakis turned us out of our huts and searched them. We know Lena betrayed you. The Chief, my husband, is very angry. She's not allowed to leave her hut. Let me help you with your clothes.'

'Thanks, Mintje,' Aunt Clara came in. 'We must look for another place to live. The soldiers may come again, maybe during the night. I don't want to be taken to the camp. I want to be here when Uncle Hendrik returns.'

'I know a place,' Mintje said excitedly. 'It's on the other side of the kopje. I often took some of the children there to play. They would examine every hole and found one that led into a small cave.' She ran on ahead, peeping into each hole along the way. Then she stopped and disappeared, reappearing again and smiling broadly as she beckoned to us. 'This is it, even slightly bigger than your old hideout.'

Kate ducked, crawled in and suddenly found herself in the cave. Maggie soon appeared followed by Aunt Clara and Mintjie. It was a close fit, but they could all stand up. Not like their old one where they had to crawl everywhere.

'This is good!' Aunt Clara exclaimd, 'even a filtering of sun can come in. We'll have to put one of the iron strips across the opening to keep out the wild life and the cave needs to be cleaned out.'

'I'll help,' Maggie burst out excitedly.

It was with a great deal of excitement that they dashed back to their old hideout to pick up their mats, karosses and utensils. Mintije and Kate carried the piece of iron. It didn't take them long, with Mintjie's help, to clean out the cave. They lit a candle and placed it in the centre of the cave to show up the uneven and jutting out stones around the wall. The stone floor also had a few spikey bits.

Aunt Clara laughed. 'We'll have to wriggle our bodies around the lumps even with the help of thick clumps of grass.'

Mintjie removed a few spider webs. One spider was an exceptionally large one with long, furry legs. Kate shuddered.

'I'll bring you some of the chief's muti to paint on the walls and on the iron you will put across the doorway. It's good muti and it keeps away snakes and spiders.'

Kate shuddered violently. Snakes were their biggest problem. They were always aware of them and had a few brushes in the past. Fortunately they seemed to be more frightened of them and slithered away when they appeared.

Kate could see Aunt Clara was happy. 'The kopje gives us a good view of the countryside, and there are so many trees and bushes around to hide it.'

'I must go now,' Mintjie told them. 'I'll be back later with some food.'

'Thank you, Mintjie,' they chorused.

They spent the rest of the morning preparing their new home, scraping out the lumpy bits of stone and sand until the floor was fairly smooth. By midday the sun was beating mercilessly down.

'Phew!' exclaimed Aunt Clara, 'I think I must rest awhile.' She sat down in the shade of an umbrella-shaped tree.

A warm feeling flowed through Kate. Mintjie had proved to be a faithful friend. That night, as they were preparing for sleep, Maggie, who was stretched out on a kaross and covered with a blanket, turned on her side and said longingly, 'Wouldn't it be lovely if we had some biltong?'

Kate's mouth watered as she recalled the delicious, salty taste of venison biltong. She could vividly remember tearing at the dried meat with her teeth and savouring the taste. The saliva built up in her mouth at the thought and she swallowed hard. As there were many mouths to feed at the huts, Mintjie could only, on occasions, bring them a piece of animal or goat flesh. They would chew on it for a long time before swallowing it. Kate pulled a face. There were still plenty of potatoes in the fields so they'll never really starve. If they were fortunate enough to live in a home again, she'll never eat another potato.

Aunt Clara's voice came to her out of the gloom of the cave. 'What do you think, Kate?'

'I don't know,' Kate replied, nonplussed. She recalled Aunt Clara's words about no one knowing of the 'treasure' buried in the coach house and that they should only use it if they were desperate and not able to live off the veld.

There followed a long silence broken by Aunt Clara. 'Maggie was so good in keeping quiet when the Khakis were looking for us she deserves a surprise. I'll go and see if I can find something special.'

'Do you think you'll able to find any biltong, Aunt Clara?' Maggie asked, excitedly.

'I'm not sure, but I'll try.'

Aunt Clara made her way out of the cave, leaving Maggie and Kate listening to the sounds of the night. Frogs croaked, insects screamed, a jackal howled. Somewhere in the distance an owl hooted nearby. Kate could feel Maggie tremble and put her arms around her.

It must have been twenty minutes later when they heard gunfire.

'Aunt Clara's been shot!' Maggie wailed.

'No, no, Maggie, don't think like that,' Kate insisted, with more confidence that she felt.

They heard the ping, ping, of bullets striking the rocks near their cave and they huddled together. A voice shouted, 'I'm going to take my section around to the left to try to outflank them and I'll want you to give me plenty of covering fire. Move your men further down the hill. You're too exposed up here.'

'Khakis!' Kate muttered, her mind in a whirl.

Maggie threw her arms around Kate and whimpered, 'I'm frightened.'

Kate tried to comfort her and stroked her hair gently. 'Ssshhsh, they mustn't hear you,' she pleaded.

The sound of rifle fire subsided and then increased with greater intensity than before. A few minutes later the firing ceased. Kate could make out a muffled shout and the sound of horses clattering over broken ground.

'Do you think Aunt Clara's all right, Kate,' Maggie whispered.

'Yes,' Kate replied, softly, her mouth close to Maggie's ear.

'Why is she taking so long?'

'She's hiding from the Khakis.'

The night wore on and on and there was still no sign of Aunt Clara. It seemed to Kate that all around the night was forbidding in its stillness and carried with it the threat of tragedy. Maggie fell into a restless sleep while Kate sat staring uncertainly into the darkness. Kate's anxiety was worsened by the realisation that, even though she badly wanted to go and search for Aunt Clara, she couldn't leave Maggie alone in the cave.

The darkness pressed heavily on her. What, she wondered, if Aunt Clara was lying wounded? A cold breeze stole into the cave causing Kate to shiver uncontrollably. She pulled the blanket closely around her. The minutes continued to pass slowly by and there was still no sign of Aunt Clara.

Her eyes began to burn from lack of sleep. Somehow or other she would have to accept the fact that Aunt Clara must be dead or she would have returned by now. Kate felt a moment of panic. Without her, how would they manage? Was she condemned to lose the ones she loved? Uncle Hendrik was away and may never come back. All she had left was Maggie.

She sat huddled up against the wall, miserable, hating the war and hating the Khakis even more. She must have dropped off to sleep because she suddenly wakened when she heard the snapping of twigs and then footsteps near the entrance of the cave.

'It's me, Kate,'called Aunt Clara, softly, as she removed the iron from the entrance.

'Oh, Aunt Clara,' Kate gasped, bursting into tears of relief. 'I th..th…thought,' she couldn't continue and her voice trailed off.

'I know,' Aunt Clara whispered, as she came in, settling herself next to Kate. 'I'll tell you what happened. I found a broken spade and dug up a bottle of something. I couldn't see what it was in the dark. Then I heard the horses and men shouting. It seemed as if all around me was gunfire. A lot of bullets came in through the coach house doorway. I dropped to the ground and crawled up against one of the walls, scarcely daring to breathe. Two Boers came in and began firing their rifles through the broken window. They did this for several minutes and then galloped away. I heard someone shout out in English, 'There they go! After them! A lot of men, it must have been the Khakis, rushed passed on their horses. I don't know how many Boers there were other that the two that came into the coach house. Gradually all the noise faded into the distance, but there was very faint intermittant firing for some time afterwards and I didn't feel safe to leave my hiding place. I fell asleep. It must have been for some time as when I woke up, even though it was still dark, I knew morning had arrived.'

'It must have been terryfying for you,' Kate breathed.

'Yes, it was, but I was more worried about you and Maggie. When there was no longer any sound of rifle shots I took the spade and dug up some biltong. I remembered more or less where I had buried it.'

Maggie woke up just as the first shafts of muted sunlight came in through the entrance of the cave. 'Aunt Clara, is that really you?' she cried, disbelievingly.

'Yes, Maggie, it's me.' Aunt Clara leaned forward and kissed her forehead. 'I've brought you some biltong and a bottle of presrved peaches.'

With that they set about the biltong and the peaches with much relish. Never had anything tasted so good before or since.

As Kate glanced at Maggie she thanked God for the way she had accepted things as they were. She seemed to understand why they had to live like animals in a hole in the ground.

From that time onwards life became more difficult. Summer was soon on them with a vengence and at night even though the heat would subside a little, the mosquitos, made sleep almost impossible. Whenever Kate was about to drop off to sleep she would soon be awakened either by Maggie, kicking and turning in her sleep, or by the moans of Aunt Clara as she tried to move. To make matters worse the summer rains came down in torrents, often confining them to the cave. Even though Mintjie had confidence in the muti of her chief, Kate knew they had to be alert for snakes and spiders and the occasional scorpion which now and again made their home under the bark of a tree close by.

One morning Kate told Aunt Clara that she and Maggie would go to the dam to look for roots and berries.

'Do be careful and don't stray too far,' she warned.

'We'll be careful,' Kate promised.

For days they had been confined to a small area around the cave for fear of being discovered by the Khakis and it was with a feeling of excitement and freedom that they ran across the veld. As they searched for roots and berries, dark clouds built up high in the sky casting the veld in gloom. Towards midday, the sky darkened rapidly from a clear blue to a threatening black. The wind came up, howling across the veld and it began to rain, not just little drops but a rushing, blinding torrent.

They ran for shelter under the broken branch of a large willow tree close to the dam. Faster and faster the rain fell and within seconds they were drenched to the skin. The storm seemed never ending but, as suddenly as it came, it stopped.

'We'd better get back,' Kate told Maggie, crawling from under the branch. 'I'm sure Aunt Clara's worried about us.'

Maggie looked at my bedraggled hair and giggled. 'You do look funny.'

Kate laughed. 'So do you.'

They ran hand in hand towards the kopje, laughing lightheartedly. The veld looked so fresh and clean. The grasses and the wild flowers seemed brighter as they swayed in a mild breeze that fanned across the veld. Kate stopped and looked about them, overcome by a feeling of elation. As she stood gazing at the beauty of the scenery, she found herself asking if it would be possible for her to live without fear? Shrugging, she gripped Maggie's hand tightly as they continued on their way.

They had gone but a few paces when they heard a familiar sound.

'Horses!' gasped Kate. 'Maggie we must hide.'

As they were still some distance from the cave they ran to a thorny shrub a few metres away and crawled underneath its spikey branches.

'Ouch!' complained Maggie, 'My hair!'

Kate carefully losened the strand of hair that had been caught up on one of the thorns. 'Shush now, Maggie.'

A moment or two later they saw a patrol of Khakis coming slowly towards them. Every now and again they would stop and search amongst the larger bushes and behind the rocks that littlered the veld. Suddenly a horse whinnied.

'Whoa, steady old girl,' a voice called out, 'Steady now Bess.'

From where they were lying Kate could clearly see the horse and its rider a short distance away, their shadow stretched out in front of them. The rider was patting the horse's neck. Kate clapped her hand over Maggie's mouth. Her heart was pounding. If it grew much louder he would hear it.

'See anything?' someone called.

The rider ceased patting his horse and looked down at them, his eyes widening in surprise.

CHAPTER TEN

Kate and Maggie stared wide-eyed at the soldier.

'No one here, Sir!,' he shouted, and galloped away.

Kate gasped with relief. They waited for several minutes before climbing out of their hiding place. When they were sure the soldiers had gone they made their way back to the cave.

Aunt Clara ran to meet them and gave them each a hug. 'When I saw the Khakis I thought the worst,' she cried, and then added in alarm, 'You're soaked through. Come, change quickly before you catch cold.'

Later, feeling warm and comfortable, they sat on a stone chewing on pieces of biltong.

Kate related to Aunt Clara the incident with the Khaki who, although he had seen them hiding behind a bush, had not revealed their whereabouts.

Aunt Clara listened intently. When Kate had finished, she looked thoughtfully at a piece of biltong. 'War is a terrible thing. Even men of peace turn into savages,' she muttered, 'but it's good to know that there are some kind Khakis out there. But how that will help us I don't know.'

Later that evening, when Kate was sitting wrapped in her blanket, resting against the wall of the cave, her mind went back to the events of the day and to the soldier who had ridden off, leaving her and Maggie undetected behind the bush. She was confused. Why had he done this? There flashed before her the vision of the sergeant and his men and how they had delighted in putting the homestead and the outbuildings to the torch.

During the sojourn in the veld her loathing for the Khakis had burned even stronger within her. In a way she found it difficult to explain. It somehow gave a meaning and a purpose to her life because in helping Aunt Clara to care for Maggie and eeking out an existence in the veld, she was showing her defiance to these men in Khaki who had brought such desolation and misery to their land.

When speaking of the soldier who had allowed them to remain undetected, Aunt Clara had said there were good Khakis. Were there more good Khakis than bad Khakis, she wondered.

Whatever the answer to that question might be they had all, both good and bad, brought misery to them. Could the Boers ever win against this horde that had descended upon them from far away or would the war continue to fester until the Boers finally collapsed under the mass of Khakis apposing them? Confused and exhausted, Kate fell into a deep sleep.

When she awoke, her head ached, her throat was sore and she felt thirsty.

Aunt Clara gave her some water and told her to rest. When she tried to open her eyes everything blurred, then cleared, then blurred again. Later the pain in her head became almost unbearable.

As she lay on the hard floor with her eyes closed, there came to her an overwhelming longing to see her mother and father again. Within a few hours the fever grew worse. She could hear the occasional murmuring of voices. Opening her eyes she tried to sit up but her head spun dizzily and everything became blurred and grey. The greyness turned to black and she felt herself falling. She found herself in a beautiful garden. The air was cool and fragrant with the heavy scent of blossoms. She began walking. The further she walked the more beautiful the garden became. Ahead of her was shrouded in mist. She was able to make out a wooden bridge spanning a narrow stream.

Stopping for a moment she looked about her. Everything was so peaceful. She walked on and was about to step on to the bridge when she stopped and stared in surprise. On the other side stood her mother and father. They were smiling.

She gave a cry of delight. 'Mama! Papa!' she called, excitedly.

Papa held up his hand. 'Don't cross the bridge, Kate,' he called. 'It isn't time for you to come here.'

'Oh, do let me come to you,' she pleaded.

Papa slowly shook his head. 'You must go back and look after Maggie.'

With that they turned and walked away, arm in arm, into the mist.

'Kate! Kate!'

Someone was calling her name.

The garden was so peaceful and cool.

'Kate!' The voice called again, this time with a greater urgency.

It was Aunt Clara.

She opened her eyes. Everything was still blurred but gradually she was able to make out Aunt Clara peering down anxiously at her.

'What happened? I don't understand,'she whispered.

'Oh, thank God, you've come back!' exclaimed Aunt Clara, kissing her on the forehead. 'You've been delirious for two days. Mintjie and I have been force feeding you with herbs and medicine but a few minutes ago I thought we'd lost you.'

Kate stared uncomprehendingly about her.

Mintjie and Maggie came into the cave.

'You better!' exclaimed Mintjie, delightedly.

'Oh, Kate!' cried Maggie, putting her arms around her.

Kate smiled. 'Yes, I'm better.'

Within a week she was strong enough to walk in the veld and dig for roots.

Thereafter the days and weeks passed uneventfully by. Occasionally, they would see a patrol of Khakis in the distance and took cover until they were gone.

Early one afternoon, in May, in the year nineteen hundred and two, Aunt Clara, Maggie and Kate, went for a walk in the fields and made their way to the burnt out homestead.

Suddenly Kate noticed a tall, bearded Boer standing near the coach house looking uncertainly about him. There was something vaguely familiar in the way he stroked his beard.

'Look, Aunt Clara!' she shouted, pointing.

'My God, it's my man!'

As Aunt Clara ran towards him he saw her and shouted, 'Clara! Clara!'

Soon they were in each others arms. Aunt Clara began to sob uncontrollably. As Maggie and Kate came up to Uncle Hendrik he gently released Aunt Clara and bent down and embraced them.

'My children,' he muttered, tears welling up in his eyes. 'I hardly dared hope that you'd still be alive. There were stories about women and children in a camp at Bloemfontein dying like flies.' Putting his arm around Aunt Clara's waist and smiling down at Maggie and Kate, he added, 'All that matters now is that the war is over and, even though we lost, we are together again.'

'But we haven't a home,' began Maggie, her lips trembling.

'Yes we have,' smiled Uncle Hendrik. 'A home is a family, it's just that we haven't a house.'

'Yes,' Kate agreed with emphasis. 'We are together again and that's all that matters.'

Aunt Clara looked intently at Uncle Hendrik. 'You say the war is lost?'

He nodded, sadly.

Maggie tugged at his trouser leg and looked up at him with arms outstretched. Uncle Hendrik bent down and picked her up. For a moment Kate thought he was going to burst into tears but his face brightened and he smiled.

Later Maggie went with Kate to fetch their belongings from the cave. When they returned to the homestead it was a hive of activity. A few labourers had salvaged some sheets of iron and were scrubbing them down. When this was done they put the sheets over the bedrooms of the small house.

Kate smiled to herself when she looked around at the workers. Uncle Hendrik was once more in charge and everything would come right again. Slowly it dawned on her that life in the cave was over. A new life lay waiting for them.

'At least the walls are intact and, if we have enough iron,' Uncle Hendrik told them, 'we'll put it over the kitchen. Mintjie said she'll bring the women early tomorrow morning to rub the walls and the floor with clay and cow dung. We have enough food for supper tonight, but early tomorrow I'll saddle up the horse and go into Bloemfontein to buy a few supplies. I'll also try to hire a small cart.'

'Hendrik, there's something we haven't told you,' Aunt Clara said, smiling mysteriously.

Uncle Hendrik held up his hands in mock horror. 'If it's bad news I don't want to hear it.'

Kate knew what Aunt Clara had in mind to tell him and she burst out, 'No, Uncle Hendrik. 'It's good news.'

Aunt Clara explained. 'After the Khakis first came, that was when they took all our livestock. Kate and I dug a deep trench in the coach house and buried most of my bottling of fruit, jam and such like, also a purse full of gold coins. We've used very little of our buried treasure.'

Uncle Hendrik stared at her, his mouth dropped open in amazement. 'Why, that's great!' he exclaimed. 'How clever of you to think of it. Our lives will certainly be made easier because of this.'

Later, as they were sitting on the floor of what had once been the kitchen eating their meal, Aunt Clara asked, 'Hendrik, what was the worst thing for you?'

He thought carefully before replying, 'Towards the end of the war I became frightened, very frightened, of myself. It was coming to the stage that I no longer felt any compassion when I saw my comrades being killed or wounded. At the start I was sickened, but living constantly with death and dying, I began to feel nothing.' He paused, and then continued, 'But the worst thing, yes the worst thing of all, was not knowing where you and the children were. I didn't even know if you were still alive. I think that was partly the cause of the downfall of the Boers, the suffering of our women and children and not knowing if they were safe.'

Aunt Clara sighed. 'The war and the suffering was for nothing.'

Kate looked curiously at Uncle Hendrik wondering what he was going to say.

'No, don't say that Clara. We fought for what we believed in and I'm not ashamed of that. Yesterday has gone. We will begin again. For our own sakes we must forgive and forget. Others have not only lost their farms but their families too. We are fortunate.'

Kate almost choked as a great tenderness for Uncle Hendrik and Aunt Clara came into her heart and, despite the ruin and desolation around her, felt a strong sense of homecoming. A bird on a nearby branch burst into a fanfare of song as if to welcome us back. Those long months, so full of unhappiness and uncertainty, now seemed unreal and far back in the past.

After they had eaten, they rose to their feet and walked into the living room. At the opening, where there had been a fine oak door, stood the Chief, Mintjie's husband.

'Hello, Gobota!' greeted Uncle Hendrik.

Gobota hung his head as if in shame. With eyes downcast he said, 'I've come to tell you that some of my children helped the British soldiers and now they're frightened to come back to the huts.'

Uncle Hendrik broke in. 'They did that to help your people.'

'Yes, yes,' agreed Gobota, hastily.

'Mintjie helped us,' put in Aunt Clara.

'The British are no longer my enemies,' Uncle Hendrik told Gabota, quietly, and held out his hand.

Kate was nonplussed. How could he say such a thing when all around them was devasation caused by the soldiers?

A smile played around the black man's mouth as he took Uncle Hendrik's hand in both of his. 'Thank you! Thank you!' he said, and hurried away.

A few minutes later three black men arrived. One held a lantern, another led a cow and the other had a large parcel of food and blankets. All these they handed to Uncle Hendrik and Aunt Clara, who stared at them nonplussed. 'Thank you,' Aunt Clara gasped.

Smiling broadly, they left.

When they had gone, Aunt Clara exclaimed! 'Soon we'll make our own butter again.'

During the next few days Uncle Hendrik rose early and journeyed to Bloemfontein. He managed to hire a small cart from a man in the town to which he harnessed Geduld, the mare he had ridden during the war, and with the coins Aunt Clara had buried, he returned with bedding, furniture, crockery, clothing and food. He also purchased enough iron and wood to erect a strong roof over the small house.

After two weeks they acquired, after bargaining with neighbouring blacks, four sheep, two goats and a dozen chickens. Aunt Clara sold some of the jars of jam and bottled fruit and bought material, cotton and an old sewing machine.

She announced: 'First Kate and Maggie must have new clothes and then I'll make pinafores and crochet doileys and tablecloths for sale. That will bring in some money until we can get the farm going again.

Kate swallowed a lump that came to her throat as she looked at Aunt Clara's very dear and tender face, shining from excitement and expectation.

'I can help,' Kate offered, gulping.

Aunt Clara smiled. 'So you can.'

After the small house was repaired, Uncle Hendrik and the labourers began preparing the land for the planting season.

Aunt Clara and Kate worked hard at sewing and crocheting and they soon had a pile of goods for Uncle Hendrik to take to the market. After buying more material and cotton for their needs they still managed to retain a substantial part of the profit.

'At this rate,' laughed Uncle Hendrik, 'I'll be able to retire and leave the money making to you.'

Kate smiled but knew he had a long way to go before the farm would make any money. At least they had enough food to eat and their home, though sparsely furnished, was comfortable enough. But it was good to see Uncle Hendrik relaxed and happy once more. Suddenly Kate wantd to shout out with joy. Maybe there had to be dark and gloomy times so that they could fully enjoy the bright sun when it came.

Early in September, a week after Kate's seventeenth birthday, she asked Maggie if she would like to take a walk into the veld. Maggie eagerly accepted.

It was a beautiful day. A breeze fanned softly across the grass. From the thorn trees there came to them the coo-coo-roo, coo-coo-roo of the turtle dove. All around them stretched the endless veld and strips of ploughed fields.

They had left Aunt Clara sewing pinafores. Since early morning Uncle Hendrik had been working in the lands.

Maggie, who had ben silent since they had left the house, began to run her fingers impatiently through her curly brown hair.

'What's the matter, Maggie,' Kate asked.

'My hair's always full of knots,' she said, irritably. 'When I grow up will I have lovely thick hair like yours?'

Kate smiled. 'Maggie, you have lovely curly hair, not straight like mine.'

With their more contented lifestyle and the good food they now enjoyed, Maggie was aglow with health and vitality. She had grown considerably and would soon catch up with Kate in height.

Suddenly, a guinea fowl rose noisily into the air a few metres away.

Maggie laughed, her irritation forgotten. 'Remember how excited Mama was when we caught our first guinea fowl?'

'Mama?' Kate queried.

'Yes,' insisted Maggie. 'I'm calling Aunt Clara and Uncle Hendrik Mama and Papa for they are all the family we have.'

Kate laughed and nodded. 'You're right,' she told her, close to tears. 'They love us as much as our real Mama and Papa would do.'

Maggie chuckled. 'I heard Mama and Papa talking about you after supper last night. It was when you went out to feed the chickens.'

'Oh!' Kate exclaimed, her curiosity aroused. 'What were they saying about me?'

Maggie giggled. 'Papa said you were growing into a beautiful young lady and one of these days he'll have to get a big dog to keep all the young men away.'

Kate felt her face redden. Their conversation was interrupted by the sound of thudding hooves. They turned and froze to the spot. Coming towards them was a figure on horseback.

Maggie clutched Kate's arm. 'A Khaki!'she whispered.

CHAPTER ELEVEN

For a moment Kate was stunned. 'I mustn't panic,' she muttered. 'after all the war is over.'

The rider drew up to them and stopped. Kate studied him carefully. He was young. In his early twenties, she guessed, of medium height and slightly built. Strands of brown hair curled from under his Khaki helmet and his grey eyes were smiling at them with amusement. Kate couldn't but notice his strong, well shaped hands. A strange sensation that she had seen him before came over her. He could have been among the group of Khakis who came to confiscate their livestock. She shuddered, but he was far too refined to have been among the rough and uncouth group who burnt the homestead.

Kate could feel her face redden with anger. The memory of the war years was still sharp in her mind and whether he was refined or uncouth didn't matter. He was still a Khaki and to be avoided at all costs.

'I won't eat you, little girls,' he said, in fluent Dutch and then asked, 'Where's your mother and father?'

Kate's eyes glinted with annoyance and with her chin tilted high snapped, 'I'll have you know I'm seventeen years old and nobody's little girl.' She turned her head away before adding, 'My mother's at home and my father's down in the lands.'

He whistled. 'Seventeen!' he exclaimed, staring at her in amazement. 'You're so small!'

'Petite, is the word,' she snapped.

He dismounted and grinned at them, revealing a set of even white teeth.

'I'm Police Constable Kitching and I've come to pay my respects to your parents. I would like to meet them.'

'Yes,' replied Maggie, eagerly. 'Come, I'll take you to them.'

He looked at her and patted the saddle. 'Would you like a ride?'

'Yes, please,' she answered, gleefully, her eyes shining with pleasure.

Kate glanced at Maggie in disgust.

He lifted her into the saddle. Looking down at Kate she chuckled as they set off towards the farmhouse. Kate was fuming.

Aunt Clara was standing at the kitchen table pouring coffee into a cup when they arrived. She stared with consternation at the Khaki-clad figure framed in the doorway. The mug in her hand began to shake and some of its contents spilled on to the floor.

'Please, Mam, I mean no harm,' said the young man with obvious concern. 'My name is William Douglas Kitching. I'm a police constable and I've come to introduce myself to you to make sure you and your family are all right.'

'Oh, my goodness!' cried Aunt Clara, relieved. 'Would you like some coffee?'

Kate tossed her head angrily. How could Aunt Clara, no Mama, be so polite to the enemy?

'Yes, please, Mam,' he replied.

'Come, inside.' She motioned him to a chair and looked at Maggie and Kate. They took their places at the table.

He removed his helmet, laid it on the table, and sat down.

Aunt Clara placed a mug of coffee in front of him.

While he was sipping the coffee, Uncle Hendrik appeared in the doorway.

The young man hastily placed the mug on the table and jumping to his feet, held out his hand. 'William Douglas Kitching, at your service, sir.'

Uncle Hendrik stared incredulously at him. 'Hendrik Johannes van Heerden,' he replied, shaking his hand.

Kate could see Uncle Hendrik was amused for his eyes were twinkling.

Maggie giggled and then quickly put her hand to her mouth.

Overcoming his surprise, Uncle Hendrik cleared his throat. 'Sit down, Mr Kitching. Clara, I'd like some coffee.' He turned to Constable Kitching. 'My horse has a bad leg.'

'Have you any idea what's wrong with your horse, Mr van Heerden?' enquired the constable.

Kate looked at Aunt Clara and Uncle Hendrik and noticed with disgust that they were obviously impressed with the young man. Even Maggie was smiling warmly at him. Was she dreaming, for this could not be real? A hated Khaki was sitting in their home, or what was left of it, drinking coffee and being entertained by a Boer family as if nothing had happened!

Uncle Hendrik shook his hand. 'No!' he said. 'I only noticed it this afternoon when I went to hitch her up for ploughing. She's the only horse we have.'

Constable Kitching rose from the chair. 'Could I have a look?' he asked.

'Yes, please do,' replied Oom Hendrik.

He got up from his chair and walked with the constable out through the kitchen door. Maggie ran after them.

Not being able to contain her curiosity, Kate too made her way to the stable.

Uncle Hendrik untied the horse and walked it slowly outside.

'Yes,' said the young man, 'I see she's favouring her right rear leg.'

Uncle Hendrik nodded.

'If you could hold her head, Mr van Heerden, I'll see what I can find.'

Kate watched, fascinated in spite of herself, as the constable bent down and after deftly placing the lower portion of the horse's leg between his knees, he began exploring the underside of the hoof.

'You'll notice,' Uncle Hendrik pointed out, 'that she'll soon have to be re-shod. I'll buy some shoes when next I go into town.'

'I'll be passing this way in about two weeks time and will be pleased to give you a hand,' suggested Constable Kitching.

'Thank you. I'd like that,' Uncle Hendrik said, gratefully.

Kate was too flummoxed to think clearly. She shook her head and watched as the constable felt carefully behind the fetlock. The horse reared slightly. 'We're getting there,' he said. 'Ah, what's this?' With a quick movement with his hand he removed a long, white thorn.

Maggie gasped, and ran and took it from him. 'Poor Geduld,' she cried, and patted the horse.

'Phew!' exclaimed Uncle Hendrik. 'I'm glad it's that and not something more serious.'

After Uncle Hendrik stabled the horse they returned to the house.

'The horse is better now, Clara,' Uncle Hendrik told her, relief in his voice. 'This young man found a long thorn near the fetlock.'

'I'm happy, Hendrik,'Aunt Clara replied. 'We need him for ploughing.'

'Look!' Maggie burst out, proudly displaying the thorn.

'Oh, my goodness, the poor beast,' gasped Aunt Clara, then turning to the constable added, 'Your coffee's cold. I'll give you a fresh cup.'

'Thank you, mam.'

Aunt Clara placed a fresh cup of coffee in front of him.

Kate watched the constable as he sat opposite her, completely relaxed as he sipped his coffee.

Conscious that she was staring at him, he placed his mug on the table and asked, 'Anything troubling you Kate?'

'Yes,' she replied.

There was a hush in the room and Kate saw Uncle Hendrik give her a puzzled look.

'What's the matter?' the constable asked, smiling.

Throwing caution to the wind she asked, 'What did you do in the war, Mr Kitching?'

The smile died on his face as if a light had been switched off.

Aunt Clara inhaled sharply and Uncle Hendrik cleared his throat noisily.

'Oh, I....' Kitching began, stiffening defensively.

'What I want to know,' she cut in, 'is this, did you burn farms and herd people into camps where they were to die like flies? Did you do these things?' Kate's words came out loud, not like she had intended them.

'Kate!' interjected Uncle Hendrik, with obvious annoyance., 'Mr Kitching is a guest in our home and you should not ask him such things. The war is now over.'

'But the scars are still with us,' she insisted.

'The land can be healed but resentment and hatred will not bring healing to our hearts,' Uncle Hendrik said slowly and firmly. Turning to the young man he added, 'I'm sorry. I don't know what's got into her. She's not usually like this.'

It was the first time he had ever chastised Kate, but she refused to be deterred and continued to stare defiantly at the constable.

He shifted uncomfortably in his chair, an expression of complete bewilderment on his sunburned face. He looked down at his hands. 'Before the war began,' he began hesitating before continuing, 'I worked with my father in Stellenbosch, as a farrier. I shod horses, treated them for their sicknesses and generally looked after them. I've always loved horses, even as a small boy. When the war started an officer of the CMR, the Cape Mounted Rifles, asked my father if he would join the regiment as a farrier. Dad had his doubts about this as he had a business to run. Also, there was a growing family to look after. As I was the eldest of five, I joined in place of him.'

Suddenly, for no apparent reason, tears began spilling down her cheeks and she rose quickly from the table and rushd to her room. She threw herself on the bed and began to sob uncontrollably.

A while later, Uncle Hendrik and Aunt Clara entered and sat on the bed.

'Kate,' called Aunt Clara.

Kate rolled over on to her back and looked tentatively at them.

'Has the policeman gone?'she asked, a sob in her voice.

'Yes,' replied Aunt Clara, 'Maggie has gone with him to the gate.'

'Why are you still nursing hatred towards the Khakis, Kate?' Uncle Hendrik asked, not unkindly. 'You made the constable, and also Aunt Clara and me feel very uncomfortable by the rude way you spoke to him.'

Crestfallen, Kate replied, 'I'm sorry, I didn't mean to hurt you.' She wanted to say something to defend herself but her voice seemed to have stuck in her throat.

'And Constable Kitching? What about him, Kate? He was a guest in our home,' Aunt Clara said, a hint of annoyance in her voice.

Kate looked defiantly at her. 'I hate the Khakis for what they've done. They destroyed our home and we had to live like animals on the kopje.'

Aunt Clara looked despairingly at her. 'Kate, oh Kate, I too know of these things.' She motioned with her hand around the room. 'Everything, all we had worked for was destroyed, but what is the sense in going on hating? It can do us no good.'

All this time Uncle Hendrik was silent. Then, taking Kate's hand, he said softly, 'Aunt Clara and I have watched you grow into a very determind young lady. When your Mama died you were a great help to your Papa. He told us he didn't know how he would have coped without you and when he was taken, you cared for little Maggie. Also, you were often a great comfort to Aunt Clara when I was on commando. You must use the determination you possess to help you overcome your burning hatred.'

Kate shook her head emphatically. 'I can't wave some kind of magic wand and act as if nothing has happened.'

'But, Kate, we too have suffered and yet we no longer hate,' insisted Uncle Hendrik. 'We avoid dragging up the past for it serves no purpose. I prefer to leave the past where it belongs, in the past.' He paused. 'I can recall the uncertainty of those days when a few unkempt Boers believed they could take on the might of the British Empire. But it's over now.'

'I hate them!' she insisted. She wondered if her voice sounded as dead as she was feeling.

Sadly Aunt Clara and Uncle Hendrik rose from the bed and and left the room.

Kate felt a terrible sense of alienation from them and sat reflecting for a while on the months they had spent in the veld. During that time the hatred she nursed had festered and fuelled a burning determination that, come what may, Aunt Clara, Maggie and her would survive in spite of the Khakis who had desecrated their land.

They had survived, but the hatred remained. She buried her head in the pillow and sobbed.

CHAPTER TWELVE

The atmosphere at supper that evening was strained. Even the effervescent Maggie was subdued and threw her an occasional perplexed glance. Kate felt bad about causing so much unhappiness and tried to make lighthearted conversation, but failed dismally.

Uncle Hendrik was thoughtful during the meal and said nothing. His eyes remained downcast and he pecked at his food listlessly.

When they had finished eating, Kate rose from the table and began to clear the dishes.

'Sit, Kate,' said Uncle Hendrik, looking up. 'Maggie and Mama can help Mintjie do the washing and drying up tonight. I've something to say to you.'

Kate noticed the name now given to Aunt Clara, and bit her lip. Catching her breath, she nodded nervously and sat down.

Uncle Hendrik sighed deeply and said, 'Are we God that we presume to pass judgement on another?'

Kate knew his remark was directed at her and she bristled.

'The war has ended some months ago, but there's still much hatred towards the Khakis,' he continued. 'There are also those among us who hate our fellow Boers.'

Kate gaped at him. 'Hate the Boers!' she gasped.

'Yes, Kate. Some of the Boers, because they were convinced we couldn't win the war, gave up the fight.'

'Gave up!' The thought was unthinkable. His words hit her like a whiplash and she stared at him too surprised to speak.

'They are called the 'hands-uppers', Uncle Hendrik continued. 'The 'bitterenders' were such people like myself who fought the war to the end, the bitter end. There's much hatred between the 'bitterenders' and the 'hands-uppers'.'

'And you don't hate the 'hands-uppers'?' she questioned.

'No. Who is to say who was right? It's not for us to judge. Every man to his own conscience. It took courage to continue fighting. It also took courage to give up the fight. I know for I was tempted more than once.' He paused for a moment and then added, 'I can't be bothered to hate anyone. Hatred saps energy and I need all my energy to rebuild our farm.' He shook his head.

He had spoken with such simple dignity Kate began to feel ashamed of herself.

'Hatred is an evil that destroys. It's dividing our land, even dividing families. The war is over but the fighting remains in the hearts of many.'

Kate hung her head, not wanting to look at him.

'What I'm trying to tell you, Kate, is to forgive and forget. The past must be buried so that we can look forward to the future. Only in that way will we find happiness.'

Kate's thoughts went back to the burning of the farm, the confiscating of the stock and those long months spent in all weathers on the kopje.

That night she lay on the bed staring into the darkness, recalling the first time she had walked into her bedroom in the small house. Her very own room that, in a real way, was to become the store for her hopes and dreams, but they had all been destroyd.

Constable Kitching became a frequent weekend visitor. He spent long hours working either alone or with Uncle Hendrik, repairing the outbuildings. Maggie appeared to be genuinely fond of him and enjoyed his company as did Uncle Hendrik and Aunt Clara.

Kate answered him politely whenever he spoke to her so as not to offend anyone but, on all other occasions, she pointedly ignored him. At the beginning he appeared to find her attitude towards him a source of amusement but, much to her satisfaction, it became apparent that he was gradually losing patience with her. The tension between them came to a climax when he arrived one weekend.

It was early on a Saturday morning. She was alone in the kitchen kneading dough for bread. The light that came through the window was a warm golden yellow.

Suddenly he appeared in the doorway. 'Good morning!' he said jovially, 'Quite the busy girl!'

Kate stiffened. Must he insist on treating her as a child! Trembling with rage, she snapped, 'It was a good morning until you arrived!'

His head jerked back with a gesture of annoyance and with a smothered exclamation of anger he spat out, 'This is too much! Kate, I'm sick and tired of your nasty tongue.'

She couldn't think of anything harsh enough to reply so, with a tilt of her chin, she ignored him and carried on kneading the dough.

'You once asked me what I did during the war,' he went on, obviously trying to control the fury in his voice. 'Well,' he continud, lowering his voice, 'I did take part in the burning of the farms. At the start we only torched the farms of those we knew were helping the Boers and could, to a certain extent, justify it.' His voice trailed off. 'I know I can never put right what I did in helping to destroy those homes. At least I'm trying to rebuild something that was destroyed, but what are you doing about your hatred? It's eating you away. The years of hate are now over.' He turned on his heel and walked outside.

She glared at his retreating figure and threw the dough on to the table. Her heart was pounding furiously and she couldn't stop the tears from pouring down her cheeks. Angry with herself, she brushed them away and continued with the kneading.

When lunch was over the following day, she went for a walk in the fields. On her return she found he had already left.

Aunt Clara looked at her curiously and said, 'William asked me to say goodbye to my little 'bitterender'.' She spoke with some consternation.

Kate's body became stiff with indignation and she turned away.

The weeks went by and there was no sign of William. Each weekend, in spite of herself, she would glance towards the gate looking for a lone horseman.

'I miss the young man!' exclaimed Uncle Hendrik one Sunday evening. 'He's been like a son to me. I don't know what I would have done without his help.'

Aunt Clara nodded.

Kate caught her breath and swallowed hard.

'I miss him too,' put in Maggie, her lips quivering. 'I wish he'd come back.'

'He will,' Aunt Clara assured her. But Kate noticed that as she spoke she glanced uneasily at Uncle Hendrik and then at her.

No one said anything for a moment or two. Finally, Aunt Clara broke the silence. 'Hendrik, we need another horse.'

Uncle Hendrik smiled. 'My wife, I'm not complaining. Somehow we'll manage.'

'I know we will, but Geduld is getting old. Kate and I have finished a pile of sewing and crocheting for the market next week and with the money we get from it you can hire a horse.'

Uncle Hendrik shook his head and ran his hand along his chin. 'We must save what we can in case the crops fail, but you mustn't worry, Clara, we will come right. Geduld is strong and as long as we don't overwork her she has quite a few years to go before she is put out to pasture.'

Kate looked at Uncle Hendrik. The sleeves and collar of his shirt were so badly frayed they were beyond repair, mute reminders that although the war was now over, its aftermath was still with them, and would remain for a long time to come.

Among the first things Aunt Clara had done when Uncle Hendrik returned from the war, was to purchase a piece of material from which she had made a dress each for Maggie and Kate.

Yes, Kate mused, they were living in the hope of a good harvest. Neither Uncle Hendrik or Aunt Clara had uttered one single word of complaint, nor had they spoken ill of the men who had destroyed their farm and desolated their land.

'Did William tell you what he did in the war?' Kate asked Uncle Hendrik.

He glanced sidelong at Maggie who appeared not to have heard her question.

'Yes,' he replied, simply, 'he told us.'

'And what did you say to him?' Kate wanted to know.

'What was there to say? We thanked him for his honesty in telling us,' he paused and smiled at AuntClara, 'If I remember correctly you asked him if he would like some coffee and he said, 'Yes, please' and that was the last we spoke of the war.'

That night sleep was a long time in coming to Kate. She lay on the bed staring at the ceiling. Images of William floated before her. Uncle Hendrik, Aunt Clara and Maggie had said they missed him. They were always straight forward and honest whenever they spoke, but she had remained silent.

Why had William not been to the farm? Was it because of her? Supposing he did come back? Should she not try to be friends with him, just to please Uncle Hendrik, Aunt Clara and Maggie? What about me? She had a silent fear of losing another person she loved. Surely the past had proved that whenever things went smoothingly something was sure to go wrong. Is life nothing more that grabbing happiness while one can? One thing she did learn living on the kopje was that life was precious. They lived from day to day and every day was like a new beginning.

She ran her fingers through her hair. Why not live each day as it arrived, just as they had done on the kopje? Satisfied with her decision, she droppd off into a deep and dreamless sleep.

On Saturday morning, a week later, Kate rose early. The sun in the distance was a beautiful gold colour with a splash of red and patches of blue. She set off towards the dam with a basket to search for eggs. As the coop had been destroyed when the Khakis burnt the farm the hens had made their nests in the fields close to the dam. Uncle Hendrik was in no hurry to build another coop as the hens were contented enough and laying well.

While she was making her way to the dam, she saw a lone horseman. As he came nearer she recognised William. A surge of excitement swept over her and she continued on her way to the dam.

A short while later she heard footsteps behind her. She stiffened instinctively.

It was William.

'May I help?' he asked, quietly.

Relief washed over her like a warm tide. She nodded. He collected the eggs while she held the basket. A broody hen adamantly refused to allow him to search under her and pecked his finger. He quickly withdrew his hand and exclaimed, 'The next time I come here I'll have to wear leather gloves.'

Without further ado, Kate bent down, placed the basket on the ground and, with a quick sweep of her hand, pushed the hen off the nest.

They grinned at each other when they saw the nest was empty.

He gave her a smile that took her breath away. 'I've admired the way   your family has got down to the job of rebuilding your lives and what you have accomplished in such a short time,' he told her as they made their way back to the house.

'Yes,' she replied, turning her head away from him. 'It hasn't been easy, but we're managing.' She looked at him and saw the tension go from him and a smile broke over his face. It was then that she realised how good looking he was.

He stopped and turned to her. 'I would like us to be friends, Kate,' he said. His voice broke as he spoke.

She looked at him, and for a moment or two, they stared at each other. Blushing, she lowered her eyes.

'What do you say, Kate, can we be friends?' he continued, almost pleadingly.

'Of course,' she mumbled.

He looked around, a frown on his face.

'What's the matter,' she asked.

He laughed. 'The dam and the trees...' He shrugged, 'They look familiar. I've travelled so much during the war I'm not sure where I've been.'

Nothing futher was said and when they reached the stable he excused himself.

Aunt Clara was in the kitchen preparing the midday meal. She looked up when Kate came in, her face beaming. 'I'm so glad William is back. His father was suddenly taken ill and he was called to the Cape, but he has now fully recovered.'

During the rest of the day, after he had finished working on the roof of the stable, William repaired a bent plough share.

After supper that evening, there was a feastive air as Uncle Hendrik regaled us with how he managed to sell all the clothing made by Aunt Clara and Kate to a man called Abrahams, who had recently opened a store in Dealesville, several kilometres outside Bloemfontein.

To her surprise she found William easy to talk to. He had a good sense of humour and soon had them in fits of laughter. She also found herself staring at him and blushed each time he caught her eye.

It was about three months later. By this time William and Kate were good friends and Kate looked forward to his visits. He arrived as usual one weekend and after an early lunch he and Uncle Hendrik spent the rest of the day in the lands. They returned exhausted, had an early supper and went straight to bed. William slept in the coach house where Aunt Clara had made up a bed for him.

The next morning he accompanied Uncle Hendrik on an inspection of the lands. They returned in high spirits as lunch was being set out on the table. Kate looked curiously at them and turned scarlet when Uncle Hendrik gave her a wink. There was a conspiracy of sorts between the two of that Kate was sure.

After lunch, when it was time for William to leave, he asked Kate to walk with him as far as the gate.

'I'll come with you,' offered Maggie.

Aunt Clara cleared her throat. 'No, Maggie, I want you to help me with the washing up.'

Maggie frowned. 'What about Mintjie? She does the washing up.'

Aunt Clara replied firmly, 'Come, you must help me clear the table, Maggie.'

Maggie sighed and shrugged resignedly, 'All right!' she exclaimed, pushing back her chair.

Chuckling, Uncle Hendrik rose from the table and left the kitchen.

With William leading his horse, and Kate walking beside him, they past the remains of the burnt out farmhouse. Even though the sky had clouded over, the sun still shone intermittantly. When they arrived at the gate William turned and looked down at her.

'Kate....er...' he began, uncertainly.

She frowned and caught her breath. 'What is it?' she asked, looking up at him. She sensed an underlying seriousness, as if he were trying to communicate something to her.

'Besides my wanting to help rebuild the farm, there has been another reason for my visits.' He stopped and her brown eyes met his grey eyes. The expression in his was searching. Then she saw the faintest suggestion of a smile in his eyes.

Suddenly he bent down, slippd his arms around her waist and kissed her on the lips. A strong wave of tenderness washed over her. He hurriedly mounted his horse and pulled hard on the reins. The horse reared.

'Whoa, steady old girl,' he said soothingly. 'Steady now, Bess.'

He galloped off.

Kate blushd from embarrasment. Then her mouth opened in amazement. Those words he had used to calm his horse, she had heard them before, at the dam when she and Maggie were hiding in the bushes. He was the soldier who had looked at them and rode away. She felt a sense of elation as if she had just awakened from a dream.

She stared at his retreating figure. After he had travelled a short distance, he stopped, turned and waved. She returned his wave. He gave a shout of triumph and galloped away.

Kate stood for a moment longer staring about her. She felt like a butterfly that had just emerged from the chrysalis, no longer a child, now a young woman. The clouds had lifted and the farm was bathed in a gentle sunlight.

With a light step, and with a feeling of joy and peace she had never known before, she made her way home.

****

Nine months later William and Kate were married. All the surrounding farmers and their families attended the wedding. It was a wonderful day. The sky was a bright blue and the sun smiled down on them.

They went for a week's honeymoon to the Cape and stayed with William's family. Everyone was so excited to see them. Then, as an answer to Kate's dream, William took her to see the van Soelens. It was a very moving experience. She and Poppie recognised each other immediately and they flew into each other's arms. Poppie was now a teacher and engaged to one at the same Cape school. Aunt Ali was still her happy self, with a lot more grey hair. Kate was sad to hear that Ouma van Soelen had died the previous year.

Junior was in the Police Force and away at the time, but Poppie showed her a photograph of him in his police uniform. He looked so handsome and the smile she recognised immediately. Before they left they exhanged addresses and promised to keep in touch.

William had left the Police and was now working for Uncle Hendrik. They would live in the small house that had been completely renovated. The farm was flourishing and all the unhappy past was where it should be, as Uncle Hendrik had often told Kate, in the past.

****

THE BOER WAR

When gold was discovered in the South African Republic, thousands of people, mainly British, came to the country to make their fortune. They were called Uitlanders (Outsiders)

Trouble began when these Uitlanders demanded to have a vote in the country where they lived and worked.

The Boers, Afrikaans farmers, were adamantly against this as there were more Uitlanders and they didn't want to lose their country. War was declared on the 11 October 1899. It lasted for two and three quarter years ending in May 1902.

****

Word Meanings:

Bittereinders - People who won't give up until the bitter end.
Boers - Afrikaans farmers.
Hands – uppers - People who give up easily.
Khakis - Soldiers wearing khaki uniforms.
Kopje - Small hill
Vierkleur flags - Four colour flags
Uitlanders - People from another country.